WELCOME ABOARD

Boating stories for your evening reading.

By

Donald L. Boone

INTRODUCTION

In a sense, it takes someone who is a bit unusual, at least in the mind of a landlubber, to enjoy life on the water, and when their day comes to a close, or when they are swinging to the hook, they frequently have an abundance of time.

It is not at all unusual to see someone lying on a cushion in the cockpit of a boat reading, a glass of something within reach to sip on as they progress through the story unfolding in their mind at the time.

This book is comprised of short stories, stories any boater can relate to, and enjoy. Most of these stories are boating related, and are experienced by this author. Most are true, but some have been changed minutely to protect the names of the guilty. The locations these stories take place, range from the southwest coast of the United States, California, then on to Oregon, Washington, and into the Gulf Islands of British Columbia.

Our parents were concerned, our children worried, but Lyn and I moved aboard out sailboat, sold our house, and went to play. We played for nine years, the time spread over two boats, and many anchorage's. We met wonderful people, we met unwelcome storms at
sea, and we met life.

TABLE OF CONTENTS

Fishing with dynamite
I'm looking for a 'Charlie Noble.'
Smuggler's Cove
Foggy Bay
Stop All Engines
Summer Fun
Clearing Canadian Customs
Cruising, is it area, or distance
Bugs
Perfect picture fish

NIGHT LINES

I was enjoying the night air as we sailed down the faces of a long ocean swells at night in an area off the California coast. Known as Big Sur, it was also known to be rich in marine life. The marine life here often brings surprises, and because of this I had reason to call quietly down below deck to anyone who might hear me.

"Hello below." It was only a few moments when two small tousled heads popped up with one of them saying, "Did you need something Grandpa?"

"No." I said. "I don't need anything, but come sit out here with me a few minutes." The two youngsters disappeared below, then returned with wind breaker jackets on over their pajama's, and I said. "Sit over there on the low side and watch and listen."

It was only a short wait, when not more than ten or fifteen feet from the side of the boat a shiny white and black object rose partially from the water, then another, both could be seen easily in the starlit night air. As they pushed the air from their lungs you could smell their salty sea breath as it made a deep whooshing sound leaving their bodies.

"Wow what are those Grandpa?" One of the boys said excitedly.

"Those are Orca whales, often called killer whales."

"Will they hurt us?" Another said as they both backed away from the edge of the boat that they had crowded so close to.

"No, they are just traveling in the same direction we are and decided to come visiting." About a half hour later when the whales had risen many times but never quite breaking the surface with their whole body and they tired of the game, they charged on ahead easily leaving us behind. The two boys chilled by the night air started below calling back

"Night Grandpa."

"Night John, night Tom." I called to their disappearing backs. The next morning at breakfast I listened as John and Tom told their sister Elizabeth about the giant whales that eat people.

It was sometime later when Elizabeth had grown a little older and when she had learned to listen for her Grandfather's voice in the night when at sea on the boat, that she was to hear me call down in the dark of night to anyone who might be awake. It took two callings before she realized I had called.

Shortly I saw her blond hair as she emerged partially from the boat's cabin and she said "Grandpa, do you need something?"

"I'd like a cup of hot tea, but come stand with me for a minute." She came up the remaining steps in her long cotton night gown to stand in the lee of me, letting my body shield her from the cool night breeze. I said to her "Watch aft on the starboard quarter and tell me what you see."

"What am I looking for?" She said.

"You will know when you see it." I said to her.

It was only a short wait until they returned and I heard her say "Grandpa, what is that? It's drawing a line through the water." She watched in awe as the line approached us rapidly, just to disappear under the boat and to come out on the other side running off into the distance. Then another and another until there were several lines illuminated in the night's sea. Some twisting, some weaving in and out of one another. Then one came from the depths streaking to, and breaking through the surface of the sea.

Elizabeth watched as the dolphin splashed back into the sea and the line continued onward relentlessly. After the dolphins left to rush ahead with other things to do and with other games to play, Elizabeth asked, "How do they do that Grandpa, how do they make those lines like that?."

"Well," I said. "There is some stuff in the water called phosphorus, and as the Dolphins push their way through the water they get the phosphorus all excited, it's as if the phosphorus turn on a porch light to see what's going on around them and they leave the light on for awhile."

Moments later, and after the magic of the night had left her, Elizabeth went below deck and I saw the soft night light in the galley come on. It was only on for a few minutes, then it went out again and Elizabeth reappeared with a cup of hot tea. She had made the tea from hot water in an thermos bottle kept for whomever might be up at night.

“Here’s your tea Grandpa.” As I took the cup I watched Elizabeth walk down a couple of steps and look around to see if all the night magic was over. After she had disappeared back into the darkness below, I heard her say softly, “Good night Grandpa and thank you.”

“Good night Little Princess.” I said. The next morning at breakfast I heard her telling her envious brothers about how wonderful it was to watch the lines in the night.

A SUMMER WOMAN

When Lyn and I first started spending time together, she knew very little about boats, other than they were objects that floated on the water. I knew Lyn would be a potential sailor, as she likes to travel, and she is adventurous.

Shortly after our marriage, we began looking at boats for sale. Lyn didn't have the fever like myself but she showed enthusiasm. As we went to boat shows, and yacht brokers, I found she liked this sink, or that stove arrangement, that ice box, and none of the Vee berths. She did have one steadfast rule, she had to be able to stand up in the head.

After several months, we found one she liked, an older boat but extremely well put together. Various colored woods throughout, and in very good condition. The engine still had the original paint on it, very clean, and ran smoothly. I doubt if the bilge ever had water in it.

After we bought "Endless Summer" home to our small houseboat, Lyn's introduction to sailing began. We started out easy, we would motor the boat up wind, raise a small jib, and let the breeze pull us home, while we dined on cheese and crackers, cold cuts, and sipping a white wine while we enjoyed the quiet. Lyn graduated to reaching and beating in light airs, and eventually into heavier weather.

Knowing how most women hate to pack and unpack, we put sets of everything on board the boat we would need. Bedding, bathing needs, a complete set of cooking pans, dishes, cutlery, as well as extra food, should it be needed for a meal while out on the water. These items were always left on the boat. The reason for doing it this way was to make it easy to go somewhere. Whether a weekend, or a vacation.

The day Lyn learned to tack "Endless Summer" by herself, was very enjoyable for me. I saw Lyn discover a new freedom. From that day forward, I've watched her grow in self confidence, and personal attitudes. Lyn learned how to bring the boat into the wind, to get her sails up, then fall off the wind and sail away. She learned how to use the radio to call other boaters, or to arrange to get bridges open for passage through them.

She learned how to short tack through an open bridge, and other tight places. She learned how to get our thirty five pound plow anchor, with its all chain rode, into the water. To figure out how much scope she needed for holding in any condition. Also how to retrieve the anchor by herself. How to change spark plugs, points and condenser on our inboard engine. Over time she learned coastal navigation, and was ready to learn celestial navigation.

I've always been of the opinion, that to shout at one's mate, is a good way to ruin a relationship. It's an indication of one's own lack of knowledge too. I only got after Lyn one time, and we had guests on board at the time. I also apologized to her right away, and in front of those same guests. Because of this attitude, it was relatively easy for me to teach Lyn things about boating. I wanted a life's partner who enjoyed boating as much as I did. Gradation weekend arrived, not a date set by either of us, just when Lyn thought she was ready.

I arrived home from work to find the boat ready to go, and the engine running. Lyn did ask me to cast off her bow line, and as she stood at the helm, she cast off the stern line. She motored "Endless Summer" out into the open stream, and down through the swing bridge. The bridge tender had already been called, and was waiting for her.

After she cleared the bridge, she shifted the engine out of gear, let the boat slow some, raised her sails, sheeted her main, then jib, turned the engine off, and away we went. She short tacked "Endless Summer" out of the two miles of channel we were in, then fell off to run downwind toward our favorite small anchorage.

Arriving at the small bay, yet still offshore its entrance, she started the engine and while it warmed up she got her sails down and furled, pulled as much chain on deck as she felt she would need, and went back to the helm. After entering the small bay, Lyn picked her spot to anchor and checked the wind direction. She brought the boat up into the wind, took the engine out of gear, walked forward and eased the anchor down into the water. As the breeze carried the boat back, she paid out all of her ready anchor chain. She then walked aft, put the engine in gear, backed the boat down and set her hook. Lyn turned the engine off, turned to me, and asked for a glass of water. I was more than happy to get it.

The weekend passed as pleasant as any we've had. As Sunday evening loomed up, Lyn made her preparations for going home. After running the bilge blower, she started the engine and let it warm up. Then foot by heavy foot she pulled in her anchor and chain. When it was aboard, she let the boat drift as she stowed the chain in the locker, and the anchor in its chocks. She then turned the boat toward open water.

There wasn't enough wind to sail home that day, but Lyn didn't have to prove anything. She brought the boat into the dock nice and easy, as she had done many times before. I merely stepped off the boat with a bow line, as Lyn did with the stern line.

After that, things were never quite the same at home again. I would arrive home to find a note saying. "Back later, I've taken the Grandkids out for a sail."

CAT ISLAND

Island cats can be dangerous, Yes Island cats, not mainland cats. Lyn and I had picked up a mooring buoy at Hope Island, then rowed ashore in the dinghy. Where we expected to have a leisurely walk on the beach.

Well it started out that way, that is until she said; “Did you hear that.”

I began to listen in earnest, my hearing not being the best anymore. “No.”

“There it is again.” She said, and began walking toward a small pile of rubble at the western edge of the beach on the north side of the Island. I watched from a short distance away, as I was busy doing my own exploring. Actually, I was just waiting for her to satisfy her curiosity.

Oh man, when she started back toward me, I could see a small bundle of trouble in her arms. A cat no less. You know how mothers get to cooing when they pick up someone else’s baby. Well then, you know how she sounded with this older child cat. Well it wasn’t a kitten, and it wasn’t full grown, so what do you call an adolescent cat?

Of course, Lyn wouldn’t think of leaving it on the Island. She swore it wouldn’t survive, an observation gained by viewing its ribs I suppose.

I tried to argue that living here would keep the cat in its natural habitat. You know stalking deer and such.

Back on the boat, I tried to touch it, but its fangs grew to an inch in length, glistening in the sunlight. With a 'Ping' of light sparkling off the tips, kinda like those commercials on television. Its toenails, you know those pointy things on a cat's feet, were extended out toward me, it intended to gut me in one fell swoop if I got any closer. Message received, I withdrew my hand intact.

Now it had to be fed of course, could it eat something simple, are you nuts, of course not. This cat had to eat three dollar a can tuna fish. Okay, maybe we didn't pay that much for it, but that's not the point.

I have to admit it did settle in easily. Well what cat wouldn't, eating well, and getting all of the attention, I mean all of the attention. Hell, I wasn't even captain any more; I was a crew person waiting on her Majesty.

Yes her Majesty had to sleep in the Vee berth with us where she could keep warm, and where her servants could attend to her petting needs, well not this servant I'm telling you.

We were on a broad reach heading from Deception Pass, westerly toward Lopez Pass, about eight miles away. The morning was warm, the wind light, and the water quiet due to the fact that it was nearing slack high water. It was such an easy run that I had the boat on autopilot. Her Majesty was sitting on top of the coach roof washing her self, and on occasion looking my way to be certain I was staying at my assigned location. A fly or something began to bug her, and then apparently it landed just above her head on the main boom.

Could she just forget it, not a chance? She jumped up, and landed on top of the mainboom with full intentions of swatting at the fly, which of course was well on its way to safety. The sail was not tight due to light airs, so her Majesty found an easy perch.

I didn't want some dumb cat up there, I mean she could fall and get hurt right? So, I shooed her. Okay I jumped up with the intention of removing that cat from my sail. She had other plans as I got closer. It would have been better if I'd have left well enough alone.

Her Majesty saw me coming, her red eyes flashing a danger warning. Well they were red the night before when I aimed a flashlight at her on the foot of our bed. With a madman heading in her direction, she took off. Vertically I might add. Did you know cats can climb sail fabric, as well as they can climb trees?

When Lyn heard me talking sweetly to her Majesty, "(@&*$-##++^!!) Get down from there," Lyn came topside. Now I was in trouble, and it was the cat's fault. By the time Lyn got topside, the cat was clinging to the Starboard spreader.

Lyn said, "Where's that sweet little kitten?" Boy, was she under this feline devil's spell. I tried to look busy doing something important, "Uhh, forward I think."

The next sound I heard, was the sound of a mother suffering in pain with one of her children, but then it changed. You know the sound of someone who has just become possessed by the devil. That deep, dark, serious voice that means business. "YOU GET THAT CAT DOWN FROM THERE."

I mean get real, we're in the middle of a seaway, and I've got'ta go aloft, apparently the answer is yes. Trouble is, my main, and Jib halyards were in use. So I decided to lower the Jib and use that halyard to attach to the Boson's seat. Of course, as you're going up a mast with an angry mother on the winch, you better be saying "Yes dear," every chance you get.

The cat did have enough sense to stay put until I got there, but once I got there, and had this snarling mountain lion in my arms, I had to get down. Lyn is careful when I'm aloft, and she takes her time letting the line slack off as she lowers me back toward the main deck. But when you're holding onto a bundle of nerves, and that bundle wants to get loose from your grip, you hold on tightly.

I wasn't sure her Majesty was still breathing as we neared the deck. Perhaps I was holding her a little to tightly. I eased my grip when I though about having to give this toothy animal mouth to mouth resuscitation. My rescuing attempt seemed to have smoothed things over, on the part of two females, one of which I want to continue living with, the other one better behave herself. Of course, this is not a point I make with either of them.

After we left Hunter bay, on the southeastern side of Lopez Island, we stopped for a couple of days in Port Townsend. We were on our way to our berth in Brownsville, and of course the Island cat had to go exploring. When it came time for us to leave, she wasn't around. We looked around as much as we could, but we had to go. I'm not absolutely sure of this, but I think I heard a woman speaking softly as we passed by a boat moored to a side. I think I heard the words, "Oh hello, little kitty, do you live around here."

RUNNING DOWNWIND

We were running downwind from Blake Island and on our way to the Kingston marina. The morning had started out sunny, but once underway, it had started to cloud over.

Robbert, our ten-year old grandson, had spent many of his young years on one or the other of our sailboats, and could easily handle our thirty foot 'Itchy Feet,' by himself.

I, his grandfather, had left him at the helm alone while I went below to fix us something hot to sip on. We had full canvas up, and as I prepared our hot chocolate I became aware that the boat had picked up speed, yet we hadn't altered course. As I looked out into the cockpit, Robbert seemed well at ease. His eyes glazed over from watching pirates in far away places. His bare feet firmly planted on the deck, and his legs swaying to the movement of the boat, the tiller firmly held between his thighs moving only as needed.

I could see aft of us, the horizon plainly visible. "How fast are we moving Robbert?"

His eye's quickly glanced at the knotmeter, "Little over nine knots Grandpa."

"Look aft and tell me what you see."

Robbert turned, looked, then turned back to me, "It's getting a little dark."

“That’s right. We’ve got a rain squall heading for us, and we’ve got to much canvas up.”

“I could reef the main.”

“Might as well drop it. Kingston’s downwind all the way, and we might as well sail in comfort.”

“Can you help me get it done?”

I sat the two cups in the galley sink and went topside. “I’ll round her up.” He said to me. He pulled the tiller over, and let the jib backwind while I dropped the mainsail, and tied it to the mainboom.

Then he let her fall of the wind, and resumed his course downwind. The pirates were gone now, but his mind went somewhere else exciting.

I finished making the hot chocolate, took it topside handing him a cup. “Here you go skipper.”

“Thanks Grandpa.” His eye’s had a twinkle of excitement as he felt his ship under his feet racing for far away lands.

A GRANDFATHER'S GROWING PAINS

I couldn't believe the difference between taking two of our youngest grandsons on a summer cruise, and then taking one of our granddaughters cruising.

It started out badly one afternoon when we were still in our home port. I'd begun to tease my granddaughter about some trivial thing. When suddenly she broke into tears and called me "Rude" on her way to her only hiding place, the port quarter berth.

I had no idea what had happened. I looked at my wife, whose arms were folded across her chest, looking at me with that look. You men know the look.

Then I got lucky. I saw the pot on the stove beginning to boil, and said, "When's that going to be done?"

My wife Lyn, said, "In about 20 minutes."

I got up from the port settee and headed for the marina deli to buy a newspaper. Anything to get out of the danger area of falling tears. To face a grown woman with tears streaking down her face is one thing. To face a child of 9, whose face has a layer of tears you've caused, is quite another.

While walking up the dock, I searched for words that fit the situation, and they didn't describe a pretty picture.

Even my shadow made the tube worms growing along the edges of our floating dock jump back in terror as I passed. Little fish scattered in every direction. I knew the word had proceeded me.

After stalling as long as I could, and knowing that I couldn't avoid trying to explain why grandfathers tease and why they tell tale tales, I started back toward the boat. As I turned onto our finger dock, I saw in the distance a little strawberry blond-haired girl heading in my direction. Her hair danced from side to side as she skipped along, seemingly without a care in the world.

When we met, Aireanna took my hand without a word, and we walked back to the boat. I sensed I'd been forgiven. I suspected my wonderful wife had put in a good word for me.

When we got to our dock box, I hoisted Aireanna onto it, hugged her to me and was about to say, "Sweetheart, I wouldn't hurt you for the world." Before I could speak, she said, "Grandpa, your face is all stickery." Okay, so now I had to go shave.

Aireanna didn't have the interest in sailing like her brothers, but she did enjoy going somewhere on the boat. On one of our daily passages, she had been lying on the bow watching the cut water as the late afternoon sun warmed her. Then she rolled over on her back and into the jib lying on the foredeck, where she fell asleep.

She developed a knack for rowing our dinghy around, and liked the privacy of exploring with it. It's not often that one youngster from a family of four children gets time to explore as she wants without having to share everything.

She asked me what the red things growing along the edges of a dock were. I told her I thought they were called tube worms. Then I said, "Reach down in the water and touch one to see what happens."

"Uh-uh," she replied.

So I reached down, and put my finger on one so she could see its reaction. Of course it shot back into the shelter of its tube. Then she was brave enough to try it.

Later, she was showing her grandmother the new discovery. She asked me what the white ones were. I told her I thought they were like the red tube worms.

Moments later I heard her surprised shriek. She had reached into the water to touch one of the white ones. Apparently, they don't feel the same.

Aireanna, like her brothers, began to discover the wide variety of bird life around the our waterways. She watched as two eagles soared near the boat. Binoculars provided a closer view of things than she was used to, so she used them often.

Grandchildren on board are indeed a pleasure. Their fresh way of seeing things brings pleasure to a grandparent who has grown accustomed to the surroundings and takes them for granted.

THE FEVER

I'm telling you it's dangerous to purchase a boat, and I know you're thinking, "What color is the sky in his world," but here's the danger, and it can happen to you.

It starts out with You walking the docks looking at boats, and something unforeseen happens, it's the fever coming over you. It can't be seen with the naked eye, but it is a contagious disease. It begins to simply take over your mind, and your body.

The best ways to avoid catching the fever, is to avoid reading boat advertisements, you shouldn't visit Yacht Broker offices, and stay completely away from boat docks. One of the more dangerous areas, especially if you catch the fever, is going into a Chandlery.

The symptoms of the fever are recognizable, in fact you may have known someone with them. I say "have" because if the fever has taken them, they are no longer in your present circle of friends. Yes it really is that dangerous, let me explain a little further.

When the fever sets in, you begin to love another outside the family. In this case it's not called adultery, but it can be as serious. You begin to make excuses to get away for stolen hours together, then it becomes afternoons, finally you're gone overnight.

Weekends are no longer enough time, the stolen time turns into holidays, and then you spend an entire vacation together.

Sometimes your family knows her name, sometimes they don't. Your family is abandoned, as are your friends. They suddenly find themselves wondering, "What ever happened to.......?"

If you were in their company you might hear someone say, "Dunno, Hummm, let's see, you know I haven't seem them since two years ago last spring."

Some folks don't even know if you're alive or dead. This line of thinking is brought about as they drive by your house. They see newspapers falling out of the paper box, it's evident the mail man has stopped delivering, and your lawn has turned to a large weed patch. Your car, when it is seen, is dirty.

Your wife, if she doesn't have the fever herself, is only seen occasionally at the door in her bathrobe. If your children have caught the fever as well, their school grades can fluctuate.

Your job, you remember, the place you go to earn enough money to buy your new love some toys of her choice. Now becomes an annoyance, if it wasn't for the money, you'd quit going there.

I know, this new love is provocative. She plays with your affections, tantalizes you, gives you a good time, then wants more of you, and your time. She's never satisfied.

There is even a greater danger, oh yes it can get worse, it can become a "Menage a trois." If she pulls your mate into her seductive realm, things can really get bad. Everything goes out of kilter, whole life styles can change. Because now you have new places to go together as a threesome, and the bad part is that this is perfectly acceptable in some circles.

The fever progresses rapidly if you end up anchored in a small slough, or cove somewhere. Because of the events that take place while you're there. The danger of these events come disguised, such as kicking back at the end of nice warm day drinking a choice wine, or perhaps an ice cold Gin Gimlet in the open cockpit while the out of control world spins past. Even reading this, in your minds eye, you can see the danger in this situation.

You'll find yourselves whisked away from the safety net of friends, yes the same ones who no longer understand you. Now they think you talk weird, you dress differently, you seem ...... somehow..... ah ...... well independent, as if you don't need their help, or advice any longer.

In extreme cases, people with an acute fever, can disappear for months at a time. If you could trace their mail, or credit card receipts, you'd see them coming from all over the globe. I'm telling you, life can become a continual off ramp.

So stop this insane idea before it's too late. Stop while your mind is still yours to control, stop before. . . . .Oh, hang on a second my sweety's calling me, and she's waiting for me to answer her.

"What honey. The tide you say?"

"Whups, gotta go."

SAILBOATS and WATERFALLS, WHEW

It happened the first time Lyn and I went boating in Canadian waters. The waterfall incident, that is.

Lyn and I were lying to our plow anchor in Mark Bay on the Southwest side of Newcastle Island. This is just to the East of Nanaimo British Columbia, and near the largest supermarket in these Canadian waters. We had been here for nearly a week, having come across from Garden Bay at Pender Harbour. Enjoying the warm, almost hot days as we explored both the Island, and Nanaimo a short dinghy ride away.

When you are inside most of these bays and coves, as a rule there is good bottom holding for a boat lying to her anchor. The small bay we were in has a shallow anchorage compared to much of the Canadian Gulf Islands area. Even here, we had out enough line to provide us with a five to one scope for our anchor. The extra line compensates for the eighteen to twenty feet of tidal fluctuation in these Canadian waters.

I only mention these facts to give you a picture of how much water it takes to fill, or empty the bays and coves in this area. With this huge amount of water on the move, there are also some fast currents flowing when the tide is coming in, or going out of these same locations. Seven or better knots is not uncommon, and five or six knots are often encountered.

The speeds I mention do not include the rate of decent over a waterfall, but it is faster than you want to travel in a sailboat without a choice.

One afternoon as Lyn and I were looking at our chart, eating home made cinnamon rolls from the oven, and drinking ice cold milk from the supermarket, we were discussing which way to go, and when to leave for our next chosen anchorage.

This, we decided, was to be Montague Harbour on the west side of Galiano Island. The Island to our south, Gabriola Island, would take us about four hours or better to circumnavigate just to get to our chosen anchorage. On the chart there appeared to be a short cut by using a small channel between Mudge Island right next to Gabriola, the Island blocking our path, and Vancouver Island to our west.

According to the largest chart we had of the area, we thought we could get through the Dodd Narrows, but I decided to talk to another nearby boater about going through this seemingly apparent short cut.

Frank didn't seem a bit concerned when he said. "Oh sure. You can go through Dodd Narrows, but only at slack water. Oh, and it should be high slack water."

Confident after talking to someone who knows the area, I returned to our boat and explained to my sweety, “He said we could go through there as a short cut, but he recommended we only go through at slack high tide.”

“You mean when the tide is between ebbing and flooding?”

“Yes my love, that’s the time.”

Now our course and plan of action was in place, we had only to head south. We left about nine thirty the next morning, trying to time our arrival at the narrows at slack high water. En route we noticed the smoke from the smoke stack at the mill to the south of Nanaimo, was going straight up. This is a signal to boaters in the area, that the waters of Georgia Straight’s could be crossed in quiet comfort.

This proved a deception as Lyn and I neared the end of Northumberland Channel. The waters here were also quite calm. As if all was well with the world, and it was for those who were aware of the area, we motored slowly down toward Dodd Narrows. We saw a few sailboats, and one or two small powerboats milling around the area as if they were playing a slow game of tag with one another. No one seemed to be in a rush to do anything or go anywhere.

We passed them on our starboard side as we headed for the very narrow passage. I suppose this should have been a clue, yet we continued onward.

I believe we made some comments about this situation, you know dumb comments. Like, “I wonder why they are just milling around?”

“Maybe it’s a club on an outing, or something.”

“Could be I suppose, but they should get their act together.”

When we arrived near the entrance, the water surface all over the entire area looked smooth, hardly a ripple was to be seen. Of course, when you think about how smooth the surface of a balloon is, you have to remember it is smooth because it is under pressure. In retrospect, you have to remember the edge of a cliff can look smooth until you get to the edge.

I’m not sure who said we should go closer for a better look, but it was a mutual decision to get a closer look before we ventured through the narrow channel, a channel we had never traversed before. The area around the Narrows, was full of greenery, an idealistic setting that boaters enjoy. The morning air was still, yet there was something different. It just hadn’t registered yet.

Dodd Narrows, now and in my mind's eye, must have been about twenty or thirty foot across if that much. On the Port side a high rocky wall dropped some sixty or so feet to the east side of the opening, with very unhealthy looking rocky rubble along the surface on both sides. When you look at these conditions, you know you do not want to get very close to them.

To make a long story short, you don't move a thirty foot sailboat up to the rim of a waterfall to take a peek over the edge. When we were getting close, at idle engine speed, I asked Lyn at the helm, "Lyn, you hear a noise?" From where I was standing next to Lyn in the cockpit, I couldn't see the foaming waters that were but a short distance ahead of our bow.

"Yes I do, and I think . . . " She never finished this sentence.

As it happened, the boat was caught in the last of the outgoing tidal current, there was no backing up, there was no stopping, we were going over what seemed like a huge waterfall. Actually it must have been about six to eight feet from where we started over, until we entered the lower level of rushing water.

This was an experience similar to your being anchored, and a pair of large ski boats pass you by, boats with engines big enough to tow ships out of danger. Sure, the ones you swear don't have mufflers on their engines.

Yep, those are the two, and they pass you close abeam, one on each side. Remember the wake as it slams off your beam, or both ends of your boat. The pitching, and rolling you experience, the cursing you do as they go by so unconcerned for your comforts.

The time span we spent going down the face of this waterfall was very short, but long enough to scare the holy Moses out of us.

However, it was long enough to see the rocky wall that blocked our view ahead. There was no time to curse the non existent ski boats, in fact there wasn't time to pray. Well, maybe for someone who has more practice than myself.

I may have heard a "Yahoo, ride 'em." from somewhere. Lyn denies it to this day, and I promise it didn't come from me. My knuckles were white just holding onto air, and there was no air moving in or out of my body. If there was, it would have smelled foul.

The water at the bottom of this roller coaster waterfall was now making an abrupt left turn. Our little four cylinder Atomic four engine came to life as Lyn pushed the throttle full ahead. Thank God she had her wits about her, and thought about what we needed to do. We were moving so fast with the current of the out going tide and having come down from the mezzanine to the lobby, we had lost steerage, and we needed it now.

As we regained steerage, we passed a rocky outcropping on our Starboard beam doing about fourteen knots, the fastest speed this sailboat had ever attained over the bottom. Well except for the time Lyn had the rail down doing about eleven knots over the bottom with heavy winds, but that's another story.

Later in the afternoon, as we lay to our anchor in Montague Harbour, a location that would remind one of the South Seas, we talked about the harrowing experience we'd had that morning.

"You have any idea how much water we had under our keel as we went cascading over that waterfall?" Lyn asked quietly.

Soothing my frayed nerves with a good wine. . . . yes the whole bottle, I said, "Nope, never had time to look at the depth sounder, too busy watching the scenery flash past."

CRYSTAL GLASSES

As Lyn and I had been in Martin Slough before, the two boats traveling with us followed close behind in our wake. We were staying close to the Washington shoreline for the deeper water as we entered. Martin Slough is about six nautical miles downstream from Saint Helens, Oregon, but it is on the Washington side of the Columbia river. The slough leads into an area known affectionately to boaters who frequent the area as "The Pond." On this trip down the river we were sharing a favored hide-a-way with some other boating friends.

As we led them up Martin Slough, still hugging the Washington side of the waterway entrance going around the eastern side of Martin Island, we entered the small cut into the log holding pond at mid channel.

This cut which leads you into the center of Martin Island, and "The Pond" shallows on each side. So, we've always gone in at mid channel. The lowest water level at low tide We've seen going through this short channel is nine feet. Once inside it drops off to an average of fourteen to eighteen feet of water, with a mud bottom. We've only anchored in here once, and there is some foul ground on the northwest area to be wary of. Usually the pond is full of log rafts, so these convenient and stable rafts frequently have boats tied off to them.

For those of you who have never tied to a log raft, there is usually a number of smaller logs that hold the raft together. These smaller logs have a large steel ring in each end of them, and these rings allow them to be linked together and, in a sense, corral the logs.

Once we were inside the Pond Jim and Mary tied up to a chosen log raft. Then Lyn and I rafted up to them, and Bob came along side of us. He wanted to be on the outside, because he had to leave in about an hour. He was going to take his boat down to Kalama Washington and it is just downriver another three or four miles. His wife Linda, had to work late today, and planned on meeting him there. Once she was aboard, they would come back and join us.

After Bob left, the four of us remaining decided to have a glass of wine while we chatted. Lyn and I were using some of our finer plastic glasses, but Jim went below and came back with two cut crystal wine glasses.

As he and Mary sipped their wine from fine cut crystal, Jim explained how their four crystal glasses had survived the trip on their boat from the east coast to the west coast. The four of us were still working on our first glass of wine when a twenty four foot power boat came along side of us.

Frank, and his lady Ellen, rafted alongside our boat, 'Endless Summer.' They accepted our invitation and joined us for a glass of wine. Frank, a houseboat neighbor, explained he was playing hooky today.

We carried on a general conversation for nearly two hours, when suddenly Lyn said. "I wonder what's keeping Bob and Linda?" We discussed them for a few minutes, then Frank suggested we take his powerboat and go looking for them. With us fella's in agreement, Frank went aboard his boat and started the engine. I, with my plastic glass of wine followed, as did Jim with his cut crystal glass of wine.

Frank motored his powerboat slowly down, and out of Martin Slough. When we got to the river, he pushed his throttles to the firewall, and as the boat came up on its step to run on top of the water's surface, we began to jump from wave top to wave top. As the boat left the top of one wave, the deck would drop out from under me, and I found myself airborne. Then, as the boat hit the next wave top, the deck would come back up to meet my feet, jarring me. There was no way I was going to be able to hold onto a glass of wine and onto the boat simultaneously, it just couldn't be done.

Frank's boat was one of those fancy designs that had a custom dashboard. Built into the dashboard was a small stainless steel sink. The stainless steel sink was of course jumping up and down as well. Feeling more of a need to hang on to the boat, rather than holding onto a glass of wine, I quickly threw my arm up into the air over my shoulder. This of course ejected what wine I had left in my glass, out into the realm of King Neptune. The plastic glass I had been holding was then put into Frank's bouncing stainless steel sink.

Jim evidently agreed with my decision, and followed the same procedure. Yet, when he reached forward to set his crystal glass down into the sink, the boat dropped off the top of a wave, and the top of the windshield hit the top of his crystal glass before he could respond. Instantly a large chip was missing from its rim.

Then as he reached down with the glass to place it in the sink, the boat came up. Now the bottom of the glass bowl and part of the stem, were in the sink with the other remains of the crystal glass.

With the boat bouncing merrily along at almost fifty knots, Jim and I watched the remnants of his glass just shred itself into ever decreasing shards from the beating it was taking in the ever bouncing sink.

We met Bob and Linda coming upstream, and satisfied that all was well with them we turned back toward the pond. As we entered the slough, Jim asked that we fella's not tell Mary what had happened to the glass he'd taken along for the ride.

Back aboard our own respective boats, we found Lyn, Mary, and Ellen still discussing various subjects. As Jim went aboard his boat, I went below, rinsed my plastic glass off, left it in the sink and got another clean glass. Topside again I found Jim had another cut crystal glass in hand, while explaining to Mary that he'd just lost the other one over board while on Frank's boat. She was upset, but controlled her displeasure at having lost one of their prized glasses.

Finally, Jim settled down on his starboard cockpit seat where he could talk with me. He set his fresh glass of wine on the side deck while he adjusted his seat cushion. In doing so, his elbow bumped the cut crystal glass where it rested on the side deck.

You're right. It fell over the side of the boat. Now Mary was steaming. Jim, so as not to let us think it bothered him, merely went below, and came back with the second to last remaining glass. He sat down again. Filled this glass, but didn't set it on the side deck. Instead, he sat it next to his leg on the cockpit seat.

Within two minutes, he bumped it. The glass tipped over, fell, and broke on the cockpit sole.

Mary, clutched the only remaining cut crystal glass of the original four, tightly to her chest. With blazing eyes she said. "Don't you ever touch this one." To this day, I don't believe he has.

OFFSHORE STORM

The first day at sea was pleasant. Sunny and warm, with some cloud cover and fairly quiet, yet, the seas were dark blue. That first night was also very pleasant.

With the Monitor wind vane steering the boat for us, we had only to watch time pass. As darkness began the second night at sea, I noticed the barometer was coming down and said to "Lyn we better be sure things are put away. It looks like we may have some foul weather coming up."

Endless Summer sailed on between ever darkening clouds with possible rain showers barely held in check. The winds were light, but you could sense the coming changes. Knowing you could do nothing about, it left only the choice of waiting.

As the following dawn approached and the winds had begun to increase. Lyn and I were aware that this often happens as the nearby land mass warms with the morning sun. We also knew that this was not the condition we were experiencing at this point in time. By early afternoon, we had Endless Summer's mainsail down to two reef points. We did this was done to ease the pressure on the rig and with the small working jib we had been using, was now lashed down on the foredeck.

When the dark of night enveloped us again, we were hove to, keeping the boat as comfortable as best we could in the bumpy seas. The boat was trimmed in such a manner that we were making one knot of speed on a heading of 240 degree south by southwest. On this course Endless Summer was heading for warmer weather on longitude 125 degrees. This direction would keep us clear of any dangers of land until we were in warmer waters off Southern California.

I was very glad we had invested in a reliable wind vane, even though it had been a real chore to get it set up on the stern of the boat. It was now steering the boat for us, needing only the wind to power it. The wind was blowing spray from the wave tops over the boat and she was constantly taking white water over the bow. It was very miserable outside in the raw weather with the spray stinging your skin as it traveled horizontally all around the boat.

The boats log read that winds had reached thirty eight knots as it howled through the rigging, with gusts of forty plus knots. Seas were running about twelve to fifteen feet as they were normally measured. I had to chuckle as to how waves are measured by the weather bureau, and what the sailor at sea would be looking at, was very different. The waves I saw were twenty four to thirty feet from top to bottom.

During the night, I would get up to look around. I wanted to see how the sea conditions were, and to be sure we were not in danger of being run down by another vessel. At the time, I thought, we are the only idiots out here, even though we were in a heavily traveled sea lane one hundred and twenty-two miles off the West coast.

The next morning at first light, Lyn said, “I hear water Sloshing somewhere.” This was not a good way to have a morning start, especially in a storm at sea. When you find your floor boards awash with salt water, you know right away there is a problem.

I forced myself up out of the pitching bed to begin pumping the water out of the bilge. I turned the breaker switch on for the main bilge pump. “Damn.” I said. “Something is wrong with the bilge pump, It won’t start.” Lyn leaned over the side of the bed, and said “can I help.”

“No sweety, there is only room for one of us down here.”

“Good” she said “ I still feel rotten.” I had a feeling it was bad electrical switch contacts, but I didn’t have time to check that out now. I scooped water out of the bilge in a cup, and put it into a small bucket, then into the toilet, to finally get pumped back out into the sea from which it came.

I found an almost continuous flow of incoming salt water to replace it. Not a torrent, but it doesn't take much to make ones imagination run wild.

During the storm the night before, as each large wave passed us by, Lyn and I would hear the anchor lifting and dropping in its chocks on the bowsprit. I was concerned that perhaps the anchor had beat a hole through the hull up forward somewhere while it had been thrashing about.

The water continued to come in, as I continued to pump. As Lyn was not feeling well, I let her alone unless I really needed her. It was apparent the boat was not going to sink, but with each passing sea, more water gurgled into the bilge.

During the stormy conditions that day, the jib sail on the foredeck had come loose. As I watched each boarding wave threaten to tear it to shreds, I knew that I would have to go out onto the fore deck to tie it down again.

After telling Lyn of the sail condition and what had to be done, Lyn wearily got up out of bed, even though still fully dressed, and together, the two of us put on our foul weather gear, and our safety harnesses.

Then we headed topside, to the raw weather that mother nature was seemingly holding us with in. In the cockpit of the boat we had a large safety ring installed so that we could snap a safety harness to it.

Lyn snapped her harness to it and knew she wouldn't have much to do, but it was a safety factor for her to be here in case I needed anything, or if I got into trouble when out on the foredeck. "Honey" she said "you be very careful okay."

My reply was "you know how it is, One hand for the boat, one hand for me." Then I inched my way out onto the pitching foredeck, fastening the clip from my safety harness to any item that would keep me from going over the side boat with one of the many waves that were washing over her.

Finally I reached the fore deck and frantically tied the jib down again, then I retreated aft to safety of the cockpit. As I watched the wave action from the cockpit it only took another five minutes before the jib was loose again. I asked Lyn if she would like to take a turn just for the experience. When her reply came back a sugar coated "HHOONNEEYY," and then" NOT A CHANCE," I went forward again.

This time while on the foredeck and tying the jib down more securely, and while buried under a ton of saltwater from a boarding wave breaking over the bow, I discovered the source of the salt water leak. I just happened to see where a wave washed over the deck, and some water flowed down through the hole in the deck where the anchor chain went into the forepeak chain locker, then of course into the bilge through limber holes.

After I regained the safety of the cockpit again I tacked the boat from a port tack to a starboard tack, and this took care of the problem. As now the water would flow away from the windlass and the anchor chain, rather than towards it.

Late afternoon found Endless Summer in the eye of the storm. Lyn was beginning to perk up, and it made me feel bad to have to tell her that now we had to go through the other side of the storm. Having been through many storms at sea, I was thinking of how interesting it is in the eye of a storm. Its interesting to observe how the seas are still very high but its mostly just peaks, and they just jump up every where. No pattern to them, just lots of single peaks of water every where, and never comfortable.

Our spirits were lifted some, just having the meager warmth of sunlight. We also knew that the front half of a storm was always the worst, and we were not worried about the quieter back half of the storm, as we knew it would be an easier passage.

From beginning to end, the storm lasted forty five hours. Of which Endless Summer was hove to twenty nine of those hours. For two days after the storm front the seas remained rolling, then it was like glass with little or no wind.

OVERBOARD

The wives of three families decided one evening on how their families vacations would be spent in the upcoming summer. The three wives would be acting captains of their vessels. With their husbands as crew, they would travel up the California coast by sailboat. The trip was to be from San Francisco to Tomalas Bay California. It almost ended in disaster, as a rogue wave took one of the wives overboard in a very dangerous area. An area, where lives are often lost in a matter of minutes in rough water.

The thick California coastal fog had engulfed Drakes Bay as the last two sailboats were feeling their way in through the white damp wall of fog. Joanne, Phil and their daughter Christi, were on their boat “Swift Water,” already anchored deep into the bay. Joanne was talking by VHF radio with the two boats as they closed the distance. Lyn and Don on “Endless Summer”, and Marion and Cliff on “Sojourner.”

Joanne had been helping them by radio find their way through the thick fog so they might anchor close by “Swift Water.” The ultimate destination for all of them on this trip was Tomalas Bay, many miles further up the coast from San Francisco California.

The United States Coast Pilot, a book produced by the U.S.Department of Commerce, and used by most prudent sailors, warns against crossing the Tomalas Bay bar entrance by strangers to the area?

As the area is known for its SNEAKER waves, and its bad bar conditions. This bar claims many lives, and boats each year.

The Tomalas Bay entrance opens into a long narrow and shallow bay. Once inside however, the rewards are ideal coves with small isolated sandy beaches. Each beach seems to be surrounded by many different species of trees to ensure the boater's privacy while bathing in the sun without human interruption of any kind.

Joanne, Lyn and Marion were to be the captains of this trip. They were to make all the plans, and ultimate sailing decisions. This year their husbands were just along as crew, which, a reversal of roles.

The three boats left Ayala Cove on the north side of Angel Island in San Francisco Bay about nine that morning. As they passed under the Golden Gate bridge and headed toward the open sea, Lyn, a more experienced cruising sailor, who could easily handle Endless Summer by herself, led the way out to sea.

Marion, although a new comer to sailing, had every confidence in herself and her boat Sojourner, but followed Lyn out under the Golden Gate bridge toward the open sea.

Joanne, who often sailed Swiftwater in races with her husband Phil, and their daughter Christi in the Bay area, was to have an edge. As she knew where to look for the right breeze at the right time, for speed, or movement in light airs in the San Francisco Bay area.

As it happened, after the three boats passed under the Golden Gate bridge Joanne had chosen a route close inshore, while heading for Drakes Bay their first stop on the trip. As it worked out Swiftwater'S route was the best one to have taken.

After Swiftwater put her anchor down far up into Drakes Bay, well ahead of the others, Joanne and Phil watched the heavy fog bank roll in from the sea, and over the point of land on the seaward side of Drakes Bay. They knew that Lyn and Marion would have to be very careful in their navigation to come in blind in this heavy fog. As there were rocks lurking in some areas close to shore and an old wharf left over from bygone days of the clipper ship trade and fishing in this area, plus a few other boats anchored here and there.

Offshore, Lyn watched the blank wall of fog as it rolled in from the open sea. Knowing they could not possibly beat it to the bay, she took a compass bearing on the end of the peninsula. This would give them a compass course to follow, and allow them to clear the end of the peninsula safely.

Lyn had Don call Marion on the radio, and suggest they change their course for Drakes Bay entrance immediately. Marion agreed, and both boats came about on a port tack, and a new course. As they entered Drakes Bay they could just barely see the rocky point of land, and Sojourner was following close by Endless Summer`S stern. Joanne on Swiftwater relayed a message by radio, that they were anchored in five fathoms of water.

Endless Summer and Sojourner having gotten their sails down, were now under auxiliary power and moving very slowly in the dense fog, and Lyn had Don take the helm as she plotted their position on the marine chart for the area.

She would tell him to turn left or right, while she watched the depth sounder, and keeping them on the five-fathom curve. Knowing this would lead them to where Swiftwater was anchored. It seemed to take forever as Lyn watched the depth sounder to track their position over the sea bottom.

Suddenly, Don said “Holy smokes, they are right in front of us.” Lyn grinned, knowing she had just finished a hard self-test in some touchy navigation.

Finally, the last two boats were anchored with the hooks bedded into the sandy bottom. Then with all hands settled in, the idle chatter between the three boats began on the radios. Everyone was well aware that the planned departure the following morning from Drakes Bay was critical. As the arrival at the shallow entrance of Tomalas Bay had to be timed for slack high water, the peak of high tide. Knowing that the slack water, occured when the tide is at its highest or lowest point and when the water in theory, is basically not moving in or out of the Bay, they made their plans on the time of departure.

The next morning broke bright and sunny, providing comfort to those who were outside in the cockpits as the three boats sailed up the coast. Phil mentioned to Joanne that the waves seemed a little higher than normal. He voiced his opinion that perhaps a storm may be building up somewhere farther offshore. Yet, their arrival at Tomalas Bay was timed almost to perfection as the tidal flow was almost at a stop.

Tomalas Bay faces the open sea in a manner that allows waves to build to unusual heights at its entrance. Its shallow entrance of four to ten feet of water, is its major contributor to the wave problem. At times, an oddball wave will cross the Bay entrance at an angle different to the normal wave pattern. These freak waves, as they are known, demand great respect.

Lyn and Don on Endless Summer were the elected volunteers to go in first. As they entered the Bay and passed the green light buoy number three, Lyn called back on the radio to warn the others.

Endless Summer had touched bottom. Her fiberglass hull raised on an ocean swell touched again and then was in deeper water. Sojourner and Swiftwater were then directed toward deeper water for their entrance.

After all three boats were safely inside the bay, they motored slowly south down the bay to a snug anchorage in Sacramento Cove.

Endless Summer was first in getting a hook into the sandy bottom. About forty feet off a superb sandy beach, a beach that looked as though it had been undisturbed for a great deal of time. Sojourner came in, and rafted along the port side of Endless Summer.

Then Swiftwater maneuvered into a position where she could lower her anchor off her stern, and then maneuvered along side of Sojourner and tied up. This made a raft of three boats, with anchors out in two different directions.

This assured them they would stay right where they anchored and not swing in too close to the beach. Or, any other hidden underwater dangers that might be lurking there.

For a couple of days, even as they were anchored in the lee of a small point of land that protected Sacramento Cove from the wind, everyone was aware that there was a storm raging offshore. They spent four idyllic days anchored there, pot luck dinners on a beach that was littered with various kinds of seashells. The roasting of hot dogs and marshmallows, with long walks on an isolated beach seemingly only here for their personal pleasure.

The swimming was limited, as this is supposedly a breeding ground for sharks. Many lazy hours were spent reading in the sunshine. Evenings were shared together for dinners that would often consist of fresh cracked crab and a few glasses of wine. Though seemingly short, it was a tremendous vacation. Yet, in order for them to have a leisurely trip home, the time had come to start the return trip.

The fifth mourning dawned overcast with questionable weather ahead. The departure time had been agreed upon so they could catch the slack high water on the Bay's entrance. Phil and Joanne needed some fuel for their engine, and all three boats needed some ice.

Because of this, that day's destination was to be Bodega Bay, a few miles north of their present location.

As the time to leave was at hand, Endless Summer cast her lines loose from Sojourner. Picked up her anchor and moved out slowly into the open bay. Sojourner cast her lines loose from Swiftwater and moved away as well. Phil started pulling in Swiftwater'S stern anchor line while Joanne was ready at the helm. Christi, their daughter, was below decks putting things away.

Phil pulled as hard as he could on the anchor line, but the anchor would not come loose from the sea bottom. Joanne suggested that perhaps it had gotten stuck under a rock. The two of them discussed backing the boat up to pull the anchor loose. But they decided this could present the possibility of fouling the engine's propeller with the anchor line.

Phil called down to Christi, and told her to call Don and Cliff on the radio, and let them know they were having trouble getting the anchor up. "Tell them to go ahead, that we will catch up with them".

After they received the call from Christi, Don, Lyn, Cliff and Marion discussed waiting for Phil and Joanne. It was decided among them to head out of the bay, as they didn't want to be late for slack water, and then to wait outside the bay's entrance in deeper water.

Phil removed the anchor line from its location at the back of the boat as Joanne passed him slack anchor line from the starboard cockpit locker. With the anchor line in hand, Phil walked forward keeping the line to the anchor taunt. Once on the foredeck, he tied it firmly over the bow anchor roller and to the capstan.

By moving the anchor line forward it eliminated the chance of getting it tangled in the propeller. When Joanne saw Phil's hand signal to her, she put the engine's transmission in forward gear. Then as the boat moved slowly forward it pulled the anchor loose from the bottom.

Joanne then put the transmission in neutral, allowing the boat to drift while she and Phil pulled the anchor up, then put the anchor and its line away in the locker. As Phil handed Joanne the last of the line, he moved to the helm getting them under way.

As they cleared the point of land at Sacramento Cove, Joanne, sitting on the starboard seat could see Endless Summer and Sojourner in the distance. She hadn't realized until then, how long it had taken them to get their anchor out of the bottom. Swiftwater arrived at the bay entrance about twenty minutes late. The ebbing tide was moving seaward swiftly, causing high steep swells with remnants of dying storm waves mingled in as well.

Phil was forcing the boat through this rough water, and while on top of one wave, he could see the other two boats waiting in the distance. In its movement toward the sea, Swiftwater would surf down the front of a wave and come to a halt as she tried to fight her way up the back of the next wave. Phil, being an avid racing sailor, had previously installed a small folding propeller on the engine's propeller shaft. This was done to reduce drag for racing as the propeller blades would fold out of the way when not in use under engine power.

The lack of a larger propeller was now causing him a problem. The smaller propeller lacked the amount of blade surface area to get a good bite in the water and to move the boat forward. As Phil glanced at the engine's instrument panel, he could see the engine temperature was beginning to rise. They were not moving through the water fast enough to provide sufficient cooling water to flow through the engine.

From her seat, Joanne was watching the bow of the boat, as it would occasionally plow into a wave. She also noticed that as the water washed back over the deck, the water running off the deck would tug at the sail bag containing their jib sail that was presently hanked onto the forestay. She said “Phil I think we should remove that jib before it becomes a problem.” Phil looked quickly at their foredeck, then said “I understand your concern honey, but if this engine gets much hotter, we will need to use it to sail out of this rough bar condition.” This was not a condition either of them wanted to consider, but they could do it if need be.

As Swiftwater plummeted from the top of one wave, and buried its bow into the next oncoming wave, Joanne, sitting in the cockpit with Phil saw the bag containing the jib sail get swept back, and nearly off the sail it contained.

The sea water pulled it far enough to let one of the two lines fastened to the clew of the jib come loose. Part of one line was washed over the side of the boat into the water, and began to trail aft as the water rushed by. Joanne visualized in her mind, the line becoming entangled in the boat’s propeller. If that happened at this time, they would be in great danger.

Without thinking any further, she got up and raced forward on the boat deck as fast as she dared. She managed to hold on to the boat and still get the line back aboard. With the line secured, she turned to retrace her path back to the boat's cockpit and safety.

Just as she raised to move aft, the boat fell off the top of a wave. At first Joanne thought she was just feeling lightheaded, but realized she was physically in the air as the boat fell away from under her. Then as she came down the boat lurched sideways and Joanne fell off the boat and into the cold sea water.

Phil looked up from the temperature gauge just in time to see Joanne surface, as the boat passed her by. He instinctively grabbed two float cushions and threw them back over his shoulder in her direction. When Christi heard her father yell down to her, she had been listening to the idle chatter on the VHF radio between their friends on Endless Summer and Sojourner.

"Christi!, Christi come up here quick". The tone of her father's voice scared her. She sensed something was very wrong, and she scurried to her father's side. When she was close, he said. "your mother has fallen overboard. Look behind us and keep your eyes on her while I turn the boat". '*Damn.'* He thought, '*Why hadn't they put on life jackets in this rough water condition.'*

Christi quickly started looking for her mother in the dull, dark green water. Through her tears, she could see her mother on the crest of a wave. "I see her dad, I see her. She's close to that red buoy over there".

Because Christi had spent a great amount of time on the boat with her parents, she knew her mother was in real danger.

Phil had to struggle with the helm in the rough water just to get the boat turned back. He had to turn the boat after one wave crest passed under the boat, and before the next one reached them. If the turn was not completed by then, the power of the waves would just push the bow back the way it had come. Phil's mind, as he struggled with the boat, was also on the water temperature of the sea. He knew Joanne couldn't stay in this cold water long, as hypothermia takes effect rapidly in very cold water.

Phil felt the boat shudder in the turbulent water, but he was able to force the boats bow through a wave top to complete the turn. He then caught a glimpse of the red marker buoy. Christi had told him it was the one Joanne was near.

Just as he caught sight of Joanne, the radio crackled to life with Lyn's voice. He told Christi to tell Lyn about her mother, Joanne.

On Endless Summer Lyn listened to the garbled radio message. It sounded as though Christi had said her folks had fallen overboard. Lyn calmly tried to get Christi to talk to her on the radio, so she could get a clearer message.

The wait seemed to last forever. Tension and worry ran high on both Endless Summer and Sojourner, as they waited for an answer from Christi on Swiftwater. It seemed an eternity had passed before Christi came back on the radio explaining her mother was in the water. Lyn did not hesitate, she called the Bodega Bay Coast guard on the radio's emergency channel sixteen. She explained the circumstances to the coast guard, and the coast guard who will normally ask many questions for their records, merely said "we are on our way."

Joanne was feeling the cold water sap her strength as she was being carried by the tide seaward, and toward the red sea buoy. She also knew that if she tried to swim, the cold seawater would sap more of her valuable body heat.

The buoy was so close now, if she could just grab it, maybe she could pull herself up onto its large flat area on top of the main float. She reached out frantically for the buoy, only to feel her fingers slip through the green slime on its side. Despair swept through her, as the outgoing tide pulled her away from the buoy and its safety.

Suddenly she was aware of a shape coming toward her, even through her eyes were stinging with salt water, she knew it was Phil bringing the boat to her. Yet she couldn't know Phil was having trouble keeping her in sight as the bow of the boat came up on the crest of waves. When it did, the bow would block his view of her. Each time the bow started down the wave front, he would have to find her in the water again.

As the boat came toward her, Joanne thought how huge it seemed as it came crashing down off the wave tops. As the gap closed between them, it looked as though Phil was going to run right over her. Her mind shouted out to him in the closing distance. *"Phil you're to close.... move over Phil, you're to close!!."* Then *"My god, I have to get out of his way."* The boat was almost to her, and she felt terror rushing through her. If the boat, falling from the top of a wave didn't kill her, the whirling propeller at the other end of the boat would as it ran over her. She tried desperately to swim with one arm away from the boat, the other arm still clutching the two flotation cushions tightly to her chest.

The boat passed close by, but as Phil tried to reach out for her, she could see he had tears in his eyes and fear on his face as their hands missed. She could only watch as the boat passed her by.

Christi was trying to talk to Lyn on the radio about the trouble they were in, when she heard her father call to her again. Because of the rough water, she had to fight her way up from below decks. But was again, able to find her mother in the sea.

As he began to turn the boat back for Joanne again, Phil glanced at the engine temperature gauge. It was high, but stable. His plan this time was to pass Joanne on the other side.

He could hear Lyn trying to call them on the radio, but he could not let Christi go back to the radio until they finished the turn. As she, was his only link with Joanne until the boat was turned fully around.

As Phil worked the boat toward Joanne the second time, he passed to far away. As he went by, he shouted to her to hang on but she looked subdued, her eyes were blank, her mouth opened but no sound came out. He knew her time was running out rapidly.

Phil brought the boat on the up wind side of her on this third try. He decided to bring the boat to a stop just up wind of her. The wind direction would then push the boat as it drifted down wind toward her. This time it worked, with the boat about where he wanted it, the wind and tide brought them together.

Joanne, numb with the cold, saw Phil reaching for her as the gap closed between them. She could feel the warmth in his hand as it closed over hers and he said “I’ve got you babe, I’ve got you.”

Phil began to pull her toward the back of the boat. As the stern of the boat was tilted forward, she knew it would be easier to get back aboard there.

Joanne could barely hold Phil's hand as she had little strength left, and she knew her life was now totally in his hands. Phil could feel the full weight of Joanne and her many layers of soaked clothing as he tried to pull her from the sea. He knew she didn't have much longer, It had to be now or hypothermia would claim her life. Phil called out to her, trying to encourage Joanne to help him, but looking at her, he knew she could not help. As adrenaline pumped through his system, he pulled with all he had.

Then another one of those freak waves, that take so many lives in this area, broke its wave top at the back of the boat lifting Joanne up. It pushed her up the back of the boat and she landed as a bedraggled heap in the cockpit. Only now was Phil aware of the tears running down his face, now as he turned the boat seaward to deeper, safer water.

Christi, drying her own eyes, called Lyn and Marion to let them know her mother was back on the boat. Lyn in turn called the Coast Guard by radio, letting them know that Joanne was back aboard.

They acknowledged her call, canceled their rescue boat that was enroute, and asked that Swiftwater stop at their dock in Bodega Bay to fill out a report.

Joanne climbed into the small shower that they had on Swiftwater and as she felt the water cascade over her body it felt scalding, although she knew it was barely warm. Her mind dwelt on the fact that the many layers of clothing she had on, while in the water, had aided in saving her life. As the inner layers of clothing had kept the water warmed by her body, close to her skin. While at the Coast Guard dock in Bodega bay, a doctor examined Joanne, and gave her permission to return to her boat, as it appeared she was out of danger from hypothermia.

Finished at the Coast guard dock, Phil and Joanne moved their boat to the marina fuel dock to get fuel and ice for themselves and the others. A fisherman stopped by their boat and related the story of how he'd lost his son in the same area the week before. All boaters listen to the emergency radio channel, and it was because of this, that the fisherman had known about Joanne's close brush with death.

Later in the day, Swiftwater was along side the other boats, which had anchored out in the shallow Bodega bay. They all sat around sharing a good wine and snacks, while they listened as Joanne and Phil recounted the events as they had happened.

With Christi snuggled tightly on one side of her mother, Phil's arm around Joanne, Joanne's hand on Phil's leg. To the rest of us, it was clear that the bond between these three people was very strong.

THE BAD PARTNERS

It may, or may not happen to you, but there is often the possibility of considering, even the accepting of a monetary partner on a boat. Someone to share the costs of purchasing, and maintaining the vessel, and someone with whom you expect to share the use of the boat.

In the early nineteen seventies, I, and a lady in my life at the time, sold a small book store and purchased a very nice, and well maintained 40 foot ketch rigged sailboat. We owned seventy percent of the boat, the bank owned the remaining thirty percent. Our intention in the beginning was to live aboard the boat and work long enough to pay the boat debt off. Then, like many others before us, go cruising.

About a year after we bought our ketch, we met a very nice couple in our yacht club and we took them out sailing. First for a day sail, then an overnighter, and finally for a summer vacation together. We connected mentally and enjoyed each others company. The four of us were each wanting to do the same thing, to go cruising. We spent hours discussing the best way to accomplish this feat, and the sooner the better.

Finally, on one weekend outing together, I proposed the question to them. “Would you two be interested in going in partnership with us, so we can all go cruising now, instead of later”?

They waited a few days to discuss it between themselves as this was not something one just jumps into. In the end they accepted our offer and the four of us started making plans immediately. We found an attorney who understood what we were about to do, and drew up a contract that was ironclad. The contract we settled on covered every possible situation that could arise. The amount of pay off each of us would receive when we sold the boat, what to do should a death in the family take place, a divorce, working while we traveled, boat maintenance, and so on.

I sold our car to a couple who didn't have the immediate cash money, but they promised to make car payments every month, and they did. Tom and Karen, sold one of their two homes, and their cars. The other home they leased out through a Realtor, and we went to the bank together to pay the boat loan off in full.

In the final months of preparation, we sailed every chance we got. Getting the boat ready, buying new sails, changing rigging as needed, hauling her out for a final paint job before we left late in the year. All in preparation to head south, then turning right for the Southern seas.

During the time we were making the boat ready, we spent evenings with other boating friends in our marina, a dinner here, a dinner there, and each of them offering to help us in any way they could.

Tom had to make one more trip to San Francisco for a final business closing. He'd sold his insurance business, and needed to finalize the paperwork. Susan, the wife of another sailing couple offered to drive him into the city because none of us had a car any longer. They were gone all day, but this was expected as our marina was a few hours away from San Francisco.

We never really noticed any difference in the beginning, blind because of our goal I suppose, but one day when Tom had disappeared somewhere around the marina, I went looking for him. I'd seen him go around the west end of the marina, so that was where I headed. I found him with Susan on board her boat in an awkward position. After the awkwardness of the situation eased, the two of them explained to me, that they were in love. I left the boat, stunned.

In less than a month's time, and about a month before our planned departure date arrived, Karen moved off the boat they were headed for a divorce. Our slip at the marina had already been promised to another boat, which meant we had to leave.

Instead of going cruising, six lives were ruined, and the boat was sold to fulfill the contractual agreement. Now out of work, and no home, My lady and I moved to another state to restart our lives.

As it happened, Tom was killed in an automobile accident less than a year later. Karen remarried, and I think she is happy.

So you see, if you're thinking about going into partnership on a boat, don't. It can be disastrous.

A GOOD PARTNER

You could find yourself with a most amazing boating partner if you do it right. When most boat owners purchase a vessel, they would also like a mate who looks forward to spending time on the boat with them. You know as well as I do, this is not always the case with wives, or girlfriends, but it can be if you do it right, and from the beginning.

If you start the boating relationship with your mate wrong, you may never recover from it. If you start wrong, you can find yourself with a lady in your life who stalls, or balks at the thought of going to the boat, let alone spend a weekend or longer on board.

First off, you as the skipper, have to want her to become your mate and a true partner. It's best to wait until the weather is nice, with only gentle breezes, supplying just enough wind to ghost along. Then take her out on the boat, just the two of you. Yes just the two of you, no one else should be aboard. Don't be in a hurry to get any sails up and start heeling the boat over.

If it's windy, and the boat heels, and if she's not used to it, it may scare her. Once you're out on the water, motor up wind a fair distance taking in the sights as you go. When you're far enough up wind that it will take you a decent time to make the return trip under sail, turn the engine off.

Take your time, open a bottle of her favorite wine, then produce some quality cheese and crackers and snacks she likes. Not the stuff you'd feed your friends who come along on race day, or for a ball game, but good stuff. Just before you start to eat and drink, raise a small jib. Yes just a small jib, remember you're not in a hurry, you're trying too win this ladies devotion to the boat. A little soft background music from the portable radio you brought along may help as well. With the jib up you'll have a control drift perhaps, but a pleasant trip to her.

While you're on your way back to the marina, have her take the helm. Perhaps you need to go the head? She will find it's easy to steer the boat after all. She'll find out about the rougher weather at a later time anyway. When you get back to marina, say "Boy that was fun." or something similar. You should take her on this kind of outing at least two or three times.

You should also find someplace nearby where you can anchor out, and still be in a protected area. Get there early enough so you can get the hook down and set. As the other boats come in to anchor, invite her topside to have a glass of her favorite beverage while the two of you watch the evening entertainment. That is other boaters coming in to anchor.

Point out how well each crew does it together should you see them. Sip slowly while you sit with her, an arm around her shoulder as you watch the sun set at the end of the day. Remember she likes this intimate cuddling stuff.

Get up early some summer morning while you're out on the boat for the weekend and fix her breakfast while she sips a cup of hot chocolate out in the cockpit watching, and feeling the sunrise. You'll do the dishes instead of her. Just a note here, if you don't help do the dishes at home, you're missing one of the best ways to make a good connection with your mate. Men should know that when you keep a woman in your life happy, she'll keep you happy. Wise men do these kind of things, almost without thinking.

If she wants to have an icebox on the boat to keep stuff cold in, see that she gets it. If she wants a different stove, such as one with an oven, get her one. If she wants anything, you get it, understand. I once had a boat with very bright yellow decks. Why? because my wife liked the color. I didn't care, I had a boat, and a wife who liked being on the boat with me. Of course when we anchored, every bee in the area thought we were a huge flower and would come out to investigate us.

Teach your lady about the boat slowly, teach her how to maintain control the boat while she is at the helm, and teach her how to sail the boat all by herself. She needs to feel needed, and she needs to feel confident in her own abilities. As she begins to feel the power of the boat under her feet, and confidence grows sailing by herself, tacking when she feels the need, not when you tell her too, you'll be seeing a partner who will travel to distant shores with you as well.

She cannot be coddled, she needs to be able to take the boat away from the dock by herself, and she needs to know how to bring it back. You, just acting as crew, can make soft gentle suggestions as needed. Show me one man who hasn't crashed into a dock, and I'll show you a man who never goes boating.

If you ever make the very wrong mistake of yelling or shouting at her, make darn sure you apologize right away, and in front of friends or company if they are present.

Shouting or yelling at your mate, is perhaps the worst mistake you can make. For two reasons, one is you will weaken her good feelings about you and the boat, and it will indicate that you are not a good boater yourself.

A man who shouts at his mate on the boat, is possibly unsure himself on how to do things, and how to handle the boat in times of stress. In other words, you will be showing you are a weak link in the boat. If she cannot trust you to react confidently under stress, she will not take chances and develop her own confidence.

Teach her correctly, and you'll share life to its peak, and a strong love with the woman in your life. When you do these things, you will find yourself with a mate who loves going somewhere on the boat, an adventuress, and often a better sailor than many men.

CAREENING

When we bought our boat, 'Endless Summer' she had a folding blade racing propeller on the propeller shaft. My experience as a non-racing sailor wanted it removed, and a standard two blade propeller installed in its place. Yet, I didn't want to spend the money just to pull the boat out in a boatyard just to change a prop
that might take about a half an hour.

Instead, I decided to careen the boat like they did in years past. Before I committed myself to this personally untried maneuver, I contacted the boat's manufacturer to be sure I wouldn't put to much strain on the rigging. They assured me that the boat was plenty strong enough, but they weren't sure I could pull her over far enough to do the job.

Saturday morning, my wife, myself and a couple of friends prepared to careen our boat. I went up the mast on the jib halyard, to the spreaders. When I was in place, I tied the center point of a heavy three quarter inch anchor line around the main mast above the spreaders, and securing it with a square knot.

This left the two ends of the anchor line lying on my main deck, and a small loop of line showing after the knot had been tied, of course the anchor on the foredeck had been removed and stowed away. At this point, the mainsail halyard was attached to the small loop of line at the knot, and after I was back on deck, the anchor line was hauled to the masthead. We positioned the boat between two finger piers, and the bow was tied off to a piling at one end of one finger dock and the stern off to another piling behind us.

Our main walk has an exceptionally strong beam running its length and this was selected to use in hauling the main mast down to the main walk. I used a length of anchor chain to go around this beam on the main walk, and used a nut and bolt to fasten the ends together leaving about six inches of slack above the deck beam.

Then I slipped a come-along under the chain loop, and moused the hook so it couldn't slip off the chain accidentally. The cable on the come-along was then pulled out to its full length in readiness. A come-along can be purchased at almost any hardware store, and is far cheaper than the cost of a haulout.

Using one of the ends of the anchor line, which was lying on the main dock, we hauled her mast down as far as we could manually and cleated the line off to a large, and secure dock cleat. The other loose anchor line was then pulled to the come-along and a bowline knot was tied into the anchor line at the point where they met. The hook on the free end of the come-along cable was placed into the loop of the bowline knot.

It was just a matter of cranking her down as far as we could each time with the come-along. When we did this the first time the original line we had cleated off was now slack, and we pulled the slack out of that line and cleated it off again. The come-along was slowly released, its cable pulled out to full length again, a new knot tied in the anchor line and the procedure was repeated over and over until we had the boat careened and her bottom exposed.

With a new propeller, a large adjustable wrench, a pair of long nose pliers and an assortment of cotter pins, I rowed our dinghy into a position at the stern and began changing the propeller, and while I was at it I replaced the sacrificial zinks.

Once this was finished, we untied the knots in the line used on the come-a-long letting it lay loose on the dock. Then we eased the other line, on the cleat, off slowly until the boat was upright again.

In preparation before hand, I had closed all of our sea cocks to avoid taking unwanted water aboard. Also, the head was pumped dry, and the valves closed. The water tanks had been emptied, and the fuel tank was nearly out of fuel, so that would not be a concern. All loose items were stored or removed, because odds were they wouldn't be where they had been left them before we started.

In addition, we intentionally left some slack in our bow and stern lines when we started, knowing that it would be taken up as the boat came over.

As we hauled her down, the side decks did not take any water aboard, but not enough to cause any concern.

Careening is so simple I'm surprised more people don't do it. Situations often arise where you cannot arrange, or wait for the boat to be hauled out of the water. Actually, all you need is to use some of your own ingenuity.

AHOY THE CAR

When I first started sailing, I kept my boat on a trailer that we often hauled to remote lakes or reservoirs. Even a few remote bays that were easy to get to by automobile, and these were delightful areas to sail for weekend outings.

It was on one of these outings that I beheld one of the most interesting events. After it was all over, I had a chance to speak to the man responsible for the afternoon's entertainment.

For some reason, trailer sailors all seem to want to haul their boats out of the water about three or four O'clock in the afternoon. This can be enjoyable entertainment to watch when you are not in a hurry.

On this particular day it was so crowed at the launch ramp when I arrived in my boat, that I just put the anchor down to wait it out. As I sipped a cool one, I happened to see one fellow kind of rush through the throng of other boats in his attempt to use a recent opening at the floating dock before anyone else could get to it. When he got there, he jumped off his boat, and when he had it stopped he handed the bow and stern lines to his wife as he headed for the parking lot.

Mind you, it was a hot day, and there were several boaters waiting to take a turn. Those who take too much time are frowned upon, so this guy was trying to be efficient.

He started his car, and pulled it down near the launch ramp. Arriving at his chosen spot, he shoved the transmission into park, and was about to get out to extend the trailer tongue, when suddenly, he looked into his rear view mirror.

When he had first arrived at his car and trailer, he had extended the trailer tongue so that it would allow him to get the trailer further out into the water and under the boat faster. Now however, he had stopped, but his trailer had not.

He quickly jumped out of his car, raced around to the back, and caught up with the trailer a short distance away. He had lengthened it out so far that the locking pin had not gone through the trailer tongue. Now, upset over this fiasco, he squatted down, and picked up the long, and heavy end of the trailer tongue.

Just before he turned around to pull it back to the car, and push the end of the tongue it back into the other part of the trailer tow bar opening just under the rear bumper of the car, he heard a lot of shouting from onlookers.

You'll remember I said he shoved the car's transmission into 'Park' when He'd stopped, well he hadn't made it. He had made it only to neutral. The car, now well out of reach, was on it's way toward the launch ramp.

It took four hours for a local dive shop to recover his vehicle from the depths between the docks, and boats were waiting everywhere, but I had a choice spot for the entertainment, because I'd anchored early.

MY STAR

We were anchored in Squirrel cove, in British Columbia. This is its name on the nautical chart, and a cove that is very large and could be called a bay. Yet there is a very small bay nearby that should be called a cove. This is a place of refuge from foul weather with good holding for anchors. It is also just a nice place to while away time with grandchildren on board.

Late on the second day, we were all lying on top of the coach roof of our boat 'Itchy feet' and watching the sunset drop into the trees at the west side of Squirrel Cove. The many colors of yellows, oranges and reds were giving way to the ever darkening sky and its many hues of blues, resulting in engulfing all of us into the viewing the heavens full of stars.

Randall, who was learning navigation from me on each leg of our trip, asked "Where is the north star grandpa?"

I said. "Do any of you see the big dipper in the sky?"

Robbert was the first to find it, "There it is," and he indicated the area in the night sky with his fingers. So his brother Randall and his sister Aireanna could see where the big dipper was located.

"Well" I said, "Follow the handle of the big dipper down to the edge of the pan, then move your eyes across to the other side of the pan. Now, looking at the two stars on that side of the pan, you follow a line from those two stars straight out away from the pan and you will see the little dipper. It is tilted a little differently in the sky, and the sides of the little dipper are tilted in more than the big dipper."

When the three of them had found the little dipper, I told them to look at the star at the end of the dipper's handle, and told them, "That, is the north star. While we are looking at stars, do any of you know where Cassiopeia is at in the sky?"

One of them said "Cassapea?"

"No, Cassiopea," I corrected. I was pretty certain they were unaware of what I was talking about, let alone know where it could be found.

When I showed them the stars that formed a 'W' in the night sky, I said, "Has anyone ever given you a star?"

They were surprised to hear me ask if they had a star of their own, and the response was, "You can't won a star grandpa."

Being a story telling grandfather, I replied, "Of course you can. Tell you what, Aireanna, you can have the star on the left side of the 'W', Robbert, you can have the one in the center of the 'W', and Randal you can have the star on the right side of the 'W'."

This has been years ago, but I still hear them telling friends about their own stars in the sky, and one time Aireanna was telling a friend about her star, and the other child wanted one. Aireanna said. “If your grandpa doesn’t give you one, I’ll ask my grandpa to give you one.”

FEEDING EAGLES

As the eagle came swooping down, we were close enough for the grandchildren to hear its wings swooshing through the air as it passed us by. Then when it was in position, its talons extended as it reached down to pick up the third bait fish the children had thrown into the water from the boat.

I, their grandfather, had shown these three grandchildren the eagle earlier where it was perched in a tall dead tree near our present anchorage. When I had seen the eagle, I asked, "Would you like to feed an eagle?"

Our youngest, at the time, Aireanna, eagerly said. "Me, grandpa, I want to feed it." Of course both of her brothers Robbert and Randy wanted to feed the eagle too.

Randall had asked "Can you feed wild eagles Grandpa?"

I replied "You can if you go about it the right way."

When asked, Robbert went below to get some of the bait fish we had gotten to use for fishing out in deeper water earlier in the day.

With the package open I told Aireanna, "Throw one out into the water and sit back, sit still and wait."

Even though she was reluctant to hold a dead fish, she did manage to pick it up by the tail with the tips of her fingers, and getting rid of it was not a problem.

After it had smacked the water's surface and began floating, Randall said. "How can the eagle see that little fish grandpa?"

"Well eagles can see about ten times better than we can, so he'll see it okay."

It seemed to take forever for the eagle to decide to come get the fish the first time. Finally, we could see the eagle launch himself off the tree limb into the air, he soared overhead with his large wings outstretched. The children watched as it came slowly lower watching everything around the fish, including the four of us.

The larger feathers on its wing tips stretching out independently to help it maneuver while, it held its hovering place in the sky over us. Suddenly, it made a dive toward the water's surface flaring its wings out at the last second to slow its flight, then easily reaching down to pick up the fish and carrying it away to have as a meal in its tree.

After the eagle had taken the first fish, it became only a matter of tossing out more fish for the eagle. This went on until the eagle had had enough of our fish, or had a full tummy for the time.

FIRE ABOARD
"Visions & Reality."

A few years ago, when my oldest son Michael listened to the Siren of the Sea, he moved on board a sailboat. He, like many would be live aboard's, had a romantic notion in his mind of how pleasant it would be to live among his fellow boaters on the water and in an ongoing lifestyle of what seemed to be, an open freedom.

I say romantic notion because in the minds of many that's exactly what living on a boat is, especially to those who live ashore. I believe it starts in one's childhood, you know, with tales about Pirates and stories of gold treasures, buxom lasses in every Port, and strong grog to drink. In a few cases this may be true yet today, but very few.

There are many social events among boaters that differ from those who are shore bound. These events may be something put on by their Yacht Club, or a simple chance meeting that takes place on one boat or another for a glass of something cool or just to wet the palate, whatever is the chosen beverage at that moment. A shared meal, can be elaborate or just snacks. The time spent together is what becomes important. It may be the sharing of knowledge about a favorite anchorage, or an upcoming trip to a new destination. It may also be about the coming winter months.

Michael moved aboard as he wished, of course this was after obtaining permission to do so from the Port authorities. He, like many new boaters, was surprised to find out that you often have to have an 'Okay' from someone in the Ports office to spend as much time on your boat as you wish.

After moving aboard, Michael asked me how to use the solid fuel heating stove in his boat and I told him. He asked if he could use charcoal briquettes in his stove for heating if he needed it in case of a power outage. I explained the danger of using this material in a closed boat, unless a ready air supply is available without restriction.

Of course, in most cases, there is always a ready air supply, as in most cases you cannot shut most boats up tight enough to prevent air from getting in one way or another. I also explained how little chance he had of getting through a winter on board a boat without a power outage.

It was a cold February morning when Michael called me. "Dad, I had a small fire on board last night. Can you come over?"

I was out the door before my warm bed cooled. Arriving at Mike's boat I found the hatch doors ajar, and as I stepped aboard, he motioned me to come below.

I looked at his stove, and saw the melted aluminum stove pipe leading from his stainless steel stove, up to the stainless steel 'Charlie Noble' as it exited his coach roof. I asked, "What the heck happened?" Well it may not have been those exact words, but that is what they meant.

"Well," he said, "I put some charcoal Briquettes in the stove, then I squirted some starter fluid on them, and lit them with a match. Then I closed the stove's door, and waited for the heat to arrive."

"And." I said wanting to know the rest of the story.

"Well," he said. "It arrived. First thing, I knew there was a roaring sound, and then the stove was getting very, very hot. When the stovepipe began to melt, I knew I had to put the fire out. So, I opened the door to the stove and threw water inside to drown the fire."

As Michael's father I'm telling you this story about this part of his first winter living aboard to bring the point home about how it can be if you are ill prepared to actually live aboard a boat year around. Some of the events that happened to Mike during his first winter aboard happen to nearly every boater living this lifestyle. The continual dampness, the occasional drip from rainwater seeking a lower level and it generally drips right where you, want to sit or sleep.

The need to trek up to a bathroom on the mainland when necessary, which seems to be miles away at this cold time of year, or, in trying to get your fresh laundry home to the boat in some state of dryness during a winter storm.

Then there is the winter chore of hauling groceries from your car in a fiberglass tub provided by the Port manager for your use, then down to your boat on a ramp that never seems quite right.

If you can manage to do this one step at a time, on a steep steel ramp, and still maintain control of this tub full of groceries which is filling with rain water, and get down to the docks safely, you have survived another day of living aboard a boat.

In the winters, and with a foot of snow covering everything, your footing on an undulating floating dock makes a drunken stupor seem simple. Your shoes never seem dry, and the summer months seem, very far away.

After spending one winter living aboard his boat, Mike realized the truth of how it is to live aboard. This is a truth all wan'na be live aboard's must understand. To live aboard you either love all of it, the winters, and the summers, or none of it, the choice is yours to make and sometimes it takes a winter aboard to make the choice.

What happened to Mike's stove went like this. He did place the Briquettes inside the stove, but way too many of them. He did squirt starter fluid on them. So much, that it created a puddle in the ash tray under the main firebox. He did light it with a match, close the door, adjust the damper slightly, and waited.

The starter fluid caught fire immediately, so did the puddle of fluid in the tray under the firebox. The incoming air provided enough oxygen to start a blow torch effect, (the roaring sound) and it got so hot it did melt the aluminum stove pipe.

Fortunately, he did get the fire put out, but a fire extinguisher would have been a much better choice in doing so. The aluminum-stove pipe was okay for most conditions, but perhaps stainless steel pipe would be the better choice. Fortunately his ‘Charlie Noble’ had been installed properly and did not allow damage to the coach roof.

So, when you have visions of living aboard a boat, keeping warm through the winter months, avoiding dripping water somewhere, especially the hatch right over your bed, you should also have the vision of spending the northern winter months, with you lying to an anchor in the southern latitudes.

Mike, having gotten through his first winter months and having lived aboard a boat, long enough to fulfill a dream, now lives in Idaho. He recently sold the boat and stays warm in the winter. The rain also stays outside where it belongs.

SAILING THE FREEWAY

Man, I was whistling down the road. I'd never sailed a car this fast. In fact I'd never sailed a car at all, and I'm not sure many others have either.

To start with, I had to park in the lee of an overpass to get out of the wind. Even then it had taken me nearly a half hour to just step the mast and adjust the rigging. A screwdriver passed through the hole in the center of the turn buckles, helped in tightening the shrouds, and the fore and aft stays.

I'd slid the mainsail in its track on the back of the mast, and onto the boom. Passed the mainsheet through its blocks, and tossed the main halyard inside the open window until I was ready to hoist the main aloft. Once I had it rigged, I climbed inside the car, hoisted the main, and hauled her in tight.

Ready at last, I started the engine and eased the car out to the edge of the roadway. The drivers of cars zipping past looked at me strangely, but I was patient and waited for a good opening. Holy smokes, when I pulled out onto the road, the wind caught me and I thought ai might broach so I quickly eased off the main sheet, but now, man I was on the move.

I wasn't sure at first if it was a siren or the wind whistling through the rigging, but when I looked into my rear view mirror the answer was apparent. The siren was from a Highway Patrol car just off my stern.

It was scary as I pushed the brake pedal. I thought at first I might tear the mainsail, so reluctantly I let the mainsheet out as far as I could to luff the sail. After I stopped the car, I cleated the line off on my door mirror, and finally pulled on the emergency brake handle. The highway patrolman was just shaking his head when he walked up to the open window of the drivers side door of my small Volkswagen.

He had his citation book in one hand and a pen in the other, he was ready to write he just didn't know what to write as yet. He started with the usual questions, you know, the ritual of a valid drivers license, name of my insurance company, etc. Each question and answer had to be repeated on more than one occasion because of the noise from the flogging mainsail.

When he asked me to step out of the car, there was some difficulty as I had to drop the main first. To do this, I had to open the door slightly to ease the main halyard. When I did this, the main came flying down, and you guessed it, it covered the top of the car and the Highway Patrolman.

After he escaped from under the sail, picked his hat up out of the dirt nearby, dusted it off, he summoned me out and away from this contraption. I don't recall him being to happy at the time.

However, on my day in court, the judge seemed intent to complete the process of seeing to it that my Prairie schooner became landlocked in the back yard, never to sail again.

"Mr. Boone let me be sure I understand the arresting officer's concerns as to why he wrote this traffic citation. It seems he stopped you, for sailing your Volkswagen on the freeway?"

I had to respond, as any sailor would. "I'm not guilty of the violation as it is written your Honor, and I wasn't posing any danger to anyone your Honor."

"Mr. Boone, I'm familiar with sailing, so explain how, and why you did this."

"Well, your Honor, it happened like this, I was driving to work one morning, and for some reason it sounded extra quiet, you know, hardly any road noise, yet I was making really good time. The gas gauge was barely dropping, so, out of curiosity I stopped on the side of the highway for a moment and opened the door.

The wind was right off my stern, and when I opened the door the wind nearly tore it off. At that moment it dawned on me that I could sail my car as fast as I could drive it under power."

I paused for a moment, then continued. "I know it sounds strange, but sailors will try unusual rigs just to see how they handle your Honor."

He smiled slightly, he tried not to, but he did just the same, then he said. "Explain how you rigged her."

At that point I knew he really did know about boats because he referred to my sailing car as 'Her.'

"Yessir. I'd stepped the mast of my small sailboat, uh . . It's similar to the Comet class, into a length of aluminum pipe which I fastened to a four by six mounted sideways on top of my front bumper of my Volkswagen. The upper shrouds were actually clothes line wire going to each side of the bumper.

I made the forestay out of the same kind of wire, but I fastened it to a short two by four, which I'd through bolted to the four by six. This was my bowsprit, and it stuck out from the front of the four by six. The backstay still needs some improvement, maybe I'll have to add a Boomkin, anyway the one I was using at the time ran down to my rear bumper.

I really got into the explanation to his Honor, that with it arranged this way, I couldn't tack the rig.

The backstay was in the way of the boom, and restricted me to a beam reach, or running downwind but I continued.

The mainsheet ran down to a makeshift traveler made from one of those rental luggage carriers, across the top of the car, and just aft of the rear door frame posts. There, I mounted a small block in the center, the line then passed outboard to another block, then to my window mirror as a cleat. I had nearly decided I might actually have to put a small cleat near this spot."

When I'd finished my explanation, the judge was silent for a moment. I thought he was counting up the amount of the fine I'd have to pay, then he said. "Mr. Boone, the traffic violation, as written, is for coasting you car out of gear."

I was grasping at straws, so I said. "Yessir, but I wasn't coasting out of gear. I had the car in high gear, but I was holding the clutch pedal down."

"If you weren't coasting with the car out of gear, what would you call it?

"Motorsailing your Honor."

TREASURE ISLAND

This is not the story of Treasure Island written by 'Robert Louis Stevenson.' Though, this is the kind of story, that inspires men to go on long sea journeys in search of their fortune. When I chanced across this information, I kept it to myself, as I too wanted to go look for this hidden treasure. Though, my travels by boat never led me to this island, I shall now pass it on to someone who might decide to seek this documented treasure. If so, please send me a couple of gold coins. A finders fee if you will.

This is the second most sought after treasure in the world, so you will not be the first treasure hunter in search of these riches. I shall word this information, exactly as it is printed on the document I hold in my hands, however strange it might seem. It is printed in such a manner, that I cannot be certain if it has capitol letters In key places, or lower case. Also, you will read some notation that leads one to think it was written in semi-recent times.

The paper, on which it was written, seemed old when it came into my hands, and I have had it for nearly fifty years. I will not add punctuation, as it does not have punctuation in most places on my copy, and it will appear here in a smaller font size, so as to keep it written in the same exact order as it appears on my own copy. It is as follows.

* * *

Location: Cocos island belonging to the Republic of Costa Rica

(Deserted but with snakes)
5 32' latitude N. 87* 10' Longitude W.*
Island is of rocky plateau with coconut trees three volcanic peaks west summit, grand summit (2,800), south cone (1,570) two springs of fresh water one located at wafer bay, the other at chatham bay two small streams flowing south (sometimes dry) one ending in the bay of hope, the other 3/4 mile east ships name "Mary Dear" capt Thompson, year 1820 (Sept.)

capt Thompson left the following known note to a mr keating (Nautical and travelers club in Sydney register no.18755)

Disembark in the bay of Hope between tow islets, in water five fathoms deep, walk 350 paces along the course of the stream, then turn NNE for 850 yards, stake setting Sun stake draws the silhoutte of an eagle with wings spread. at the extremity of sun and shadow: cave marked with a cross. here lies the treasure. we have buried at a depth of four feet in the red earth:

1 chest: alter trimmings of cloth of gold, with Baldachins, Monstrances, chalices, comprising 1,244 stones.

1 chest: 2 gold Reliquaries weighing 120 pound, with 624 topazes, cornelians and emeralds, 12 diamonds.

1 chest: 3 Reliquaries of cast metal weighing 160 pounds, with 860 rubies and various stones, 19 diamonds

1 chest: 4,000 doubloons of spain marked 8. 5,ooo crowns of mexico. 124 swords, 64 dirks, 120 shoulder belts, 28 rondaches.

1 chest: 8 caskets of cedar-wood and silver, with 3,840 cut stones, rings, patens and 4,265 uncut stones.

28 feet to the North-east, at a depth of 8 feet in the yellow sand: 7 chest: with 22 candelabra in gold and silver weighing 250 pounds, and 164 rubies a foot.

12 armspans west, at a depth of 10 feet in red earth: the seven foot virgin of gold, with the child jesus and her crown and pectoral of 780 pounds, rolled in her gold chasuble of which are 1,684 jewels. 3 of these are 4 inch emeralds on the pectoral and 6 are 6 inch topazes on the crown, the 7 crosses are of diamonds.

Estimated value is from ten to twenty thousand million Francs
Mr keating made three trips removing five hundred million Francs (est.) (he is believed to have only taken the smaller portable items)

Keating only notes at two cable lengths, south of the last watering place, on three points. The cave is the one which is to be found under the second point. Christie, Ned and Anton have tried but none of the three has returned. Ned on his fourth dive found the enterance at twelve fathoms but did not emerge from his fifth dive.

there are no octopuses but there are sharks. a path must be opened up to the cave from the west. I believe there has been a fall of rock at the enterance.

Note:
Another seeking in 1929 found a cave south of the bay of hope NNE of Meule island that was accessible for one hour at every low tide. Having almost lost his life by drowning after entering the cave. the tide came in filling the cave, he was only able to escape by using the undertow of the tide.

Perhaps this is what happened to the three divers above. also perhaps keating left the above not to discourage or throw any follower off the track. (nothing found)

My recollection at this time, is that these are notes from someone's research. The drawing was done on my computer, but represents the one on my documents. I can add nothing further to this information, from this point it is yours to do with, as you wish.

At one time, I did inquire on the Internet, as to any record of a register in Sydney, though I don't

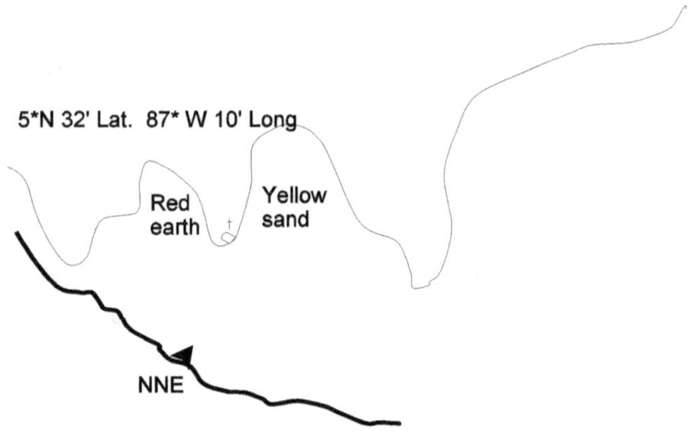

recall my findings, they must not have been rewarding at the time. Yes, I know, you are saying "Which Sydney?" I don't know any more about it than you.

Good hunting.

RESUSCITATING BIRDS

I mean I love my grandchildren, but sometimes they try my patience. It's as if they think I can do anything, I mean, . . . Well, let me give you an example.

We were in a lee where we anchored near Canoe Point, with two of our younger grandchildren aboard, the youngest boy, Isaiah, and the only girl from that part of the family, Aireanna. I had the main hoisted because it was wet from an earlier rain. The day, now warm and sunny, just perfect for drying sails.

I was sipping some really good Brandy while I made notes for one of my favorite editors Karen. Aireanna was reading a children's story about bats, or was it 'Free Willy,' well anyway she was sitting in the cockpit with me. Suddenly, we heard a 'Thwack' then a 'Thunk,' and there, on our coach roof, lay a small bird of some kind. Hell I don't know what kind it was, do I look like an Ornithologist?

I'm sorry, I shouldn't be upset, but after all good Brandy and for a bird. Oh. . .yeah, you need to know about the bird. Well you see, I'da left it there, probably just knocked out or something, but not Aireanna, oh no, she had to go pick it up, it had to be saved.

She cuddled it to her chest, cupped in her hands, and then sat down again across from me, "Grandpa, you have to help it."

I was trying to concentrate, and without thinking I said. “Aireanna, just throw the bird over the side, it’s probably dead anyway.”

Whoa, this is not something to say to a child of a tender age, especially one whose whole life is currently wrapped around saving whales and stuff. It was only nanoseconds before her eyes filled with tears, “NO, Grandpa, it’s alive, and as she put up next to her cheek, she continued with, I think I can feel its heart beating.”

Okay, there wasn’t any question I had to do something, but what? “Well sweetheart, what do you suggest?” and that was where I went wrong.

“Give it resuscitation.”

“Do what?”

“Help it breath again, you know like they do people.” Some how the bird immediately found it way into my hands. The hands of a grandfather who a grandchild thought could do anything.

Okay, it’s not like there was a crowd gathered around, so I reached into the small open space under a deck winch, and amid the winch handles, I found a small rag I knew was in there. I dipped the rag into my glass of Brandy, then began to wipe off the bird’s beak, and opening partially so I could do a good job of cleaning it before the resuscitation began. Well, who knows where this bird’s beak has been, right?

I wanted to be sure it was well cleaned, so I dipped the rag several times, and each time washed the bird's beak and now, little open mouth. Then the hard part started. I mean, if you actually blow into its little nostrils, you'd blow its lungs apart inside. So, instead I just got my mouth close to it, and puffed little spurts of air at it nostrils. Hey, it satisfied Aireanna.

Finally I'd had enough, so I took the bird and the rag, up onto the foredeck. I placed the bird carefully on the rag, still wet with Brandy, near the bow where I could kick it overboard later. Then I insisted on Aireanna's staying away from the bird so that it could recuperate.

I went back to making more notes, all the while watching out of the corner of my eyes, a nervous Aireanna trying to read, but who constantly shifted around. Her eyes darting forward to see how the bird was doing.

"*GRANDPA, GRANDPA*." I heard in hushed tones.

"The bird, it's alive, it's alive. Grandpa you saved it."

I quickly glanced forward, and I'm not foolin, that bird was up walking around. Well staggering is more like it. It stepped sideways when it meant to go forward, and it fell on its beak a couple'a times, but it got back up each time.

As we watched in awe, it began to flap its little wings and finally took off, and not in a straight line either.

The Brandy, well I'd almost decided I'd sip it, but the sight of the small bits of whatever, that lay in the bottom of the glass from who knows where, I poured it over the side. Well, Davey Jones still likes Brandy, doesn't he?

The next afternoon, a bird that looked familiar landed on our foredeck, walked around, as if looking for something, something like a Bandy soaked rag. No doubt party type bird.

CRUISING WITH GRANDCHILDREN

"Grandpa, Grandma, look at the giant Jelly Fishes." The boys were shouting back at Lyn and me from the bow, their hands pointing in every direction at once. Their young bodies almost couldn't take the constant twisting and turning in the effort to see every thing as we passed through the quiet morning waters of Puget Sound. I looked over the side as we passed through the school of Jelly Fish. They were just ordinary Jelly Fish, but not to these two city kids from Hillsboro, Oregon.

Having Grandchildren aboard is a wonderful experience and something Lyn and I looked forward to every summer. Our younger grandchildren were of the age where the things they experience are memories they will keep forever. Because of this, Lyn and I, their grandparents, try to make those memories as positive as we can.

It was August the first year when we took the two older boys, Robbert, then ten, and Randal nine, on our sail boat "ITCHY FEET" with the intention of introducing them to our boating lifestyle. They'd been aboard our boat before, but not for any length of time.

When Robbert was a very young lad, our daughter and her husband would often come visit us on our house boat on the Columbia River. Robbert always wanted to get on the boat.

He would sit for hours in the cockpit of the boat with a life jacket on pretending he was steering, something most boys do behind the steering wheel of their dad's car.

The age limit you set for youngsters on board for any length of time is arbitrary. Our minimum age limit is eight years old. We chose this age because we feel the children will listen to what they are told.

We spent the first day aboard just getting the boys settled in, letting them get used to being aboard. Actually, I was afraid they might get seasick, but this fear was a waste of my own energy. They never seemed to notice the motion of the boat at any time during their stay aboard.

As the first day in the marina passed, we explained our boating rules, such as, while we were out boating, anytime they left the safety of the cockpit they had to have a life jacket on without exception. Lyn and I had purchased life jackets to fit each of them according to their weight. Then, while in we were in the protected waters of the marina, they learned how to get into and out of the dinghy, and how to row it.

Their sleeping areas were defined and I explained that their personal belongings had to be put away whenever they were not actually in use. The reason things had to be put away, I explained, was to reduce any chance of injury to anyone while the boat was moving.

That afternoon the boys, and I sat in the shade of our cockpit boom tent drinking a cold soda pop. We were looking over the charts as to places we could explore. Previously Lyn and I had given each boy two note books. One was to keep a daily log, so that they could read it again later. It was actually done so their mom and dad could read it as well. Another, was a work book.

The work book was put to use while we were sitting in the cockpit discussing where we were going. I explained to the boys about the depth of our keel, and how much water we needed to keep us floating. I helped them draw a rough sketch of a sailboat hull in their workbooks for reference.

They were each given a tide book, and when I explained about how much the tide fluctuated in Puget Sound, they were amazed. It was hard for them to visualize how that much water could just go away and come back again.

It surprised them to learn that the tide could still be going out in South Puget Sound while it had already started to come back in at the entrance to Juan De Fuca. A new picture was drawn in their work books, this one had a wavy water line for the high tide, and one for the low tide, both in relationship to a land mass.

The main reason for doing this, was to put their mathematical skills to work, to show them that the arithmetic they were learning in school is of importance. It is something they will use every day of their lives. A new picture was drawn in their workbooks, explaining what anchor line scope was, and why it was used.

Giving them examples such as, “If we anchor in six fathoms of water, and we need at least a four to one scope, how much anchor line is that?” After a few locations were discussed, they became aware of where to look on a chart to see if it was in feet or fathoms.

Over the course of their stay on the boat, when we decided it was time to pull the hook and move on, we would discuss where we would go next. It then became a rush to see who could get the answer for the correct amount of scope needed for the next location.

They learned how to use the VFH radio, how to start the boat engine and to check for cooling water exiting the exhaust system; how to check the engine oil, and grease the engine’s water pump.

We left Brownsville, Washington in the early morning hours heading south. Canvas was hoisted aloft and when I gave them turns at the helm to sail, we all enjoyed their new feelings of freedom. They were wide eyed as they first experienced the feel and power of the boat under their feet while at the helm. They were a little afraid and nervous when they first began to take control of the vessel knowing that they were in control of their grandfathers boat. My grandchildren never tell me anymore that they can’t do something, because they know I’ll tell them they can do anything. Now they just do as I ask. Trust is a powerful tool. Use it wisely.

Our first day was a long one, perhaps an error on my part. When their grandmother took a nap on the run down to Dockton in Quartermaster Harbor, they decided it was okay for them to take one also. Randal crashed on the Starboard settee, while Robbert laid down on the Starboard cockpit seat across from me.

We spent two days in Dockton. The boys were allowed to take the dink into the county park dock to play in the children's playground. The first evening when they found out that their grandfather filled out a daily log book, and I offered to help them with theirs, and they wrote in their own log books willingly. This, became a ritual they carried out daily after that.

As we traveled, Lyn would get out her bird book and point out different birds, many of which they as city kids had never seen. A list was maintained in their log book of the many different things they saw. They spent hours at the bow watching the cut water as we moved along, often hollering out to one another at some new item they hadn't seen before.

After leaving Quartermaster harbor, we sailed north to Blake Island where we spent a few more days. When we arrived, we moored to a state park buoy just off the northwest side of the Island. Robbert couldn't believe we could just tie the boat to a tire floating in the water and expect the boat and the tire to remain in place. Once again a picture was drawn in their work book, this time with a drawing of how the buoys are built and how they are moored to the sea bottom. None the less, Robbert kept a wary eye on that mooring buoy that evening, and the next morning the first thing he did when he got up was to verify our position.

As days ended, we never told them when they had to go to bed. Darkness took care of that. They, of course weren't used to sleeping on a boat, and had been given the Port and Starboard settees as berths and their private areas at night. We used these as their sleeping areas as our stern quarter berth was used for storage of cruising necessities.

On one of our first nights out on the boat, I heard a solid kerthunk of unknown origin. I got up to investigate and found Randal laying on the main cabin sole. He hadn't even awakened when he fell off the settee. I left him there.

Whenever we were near a telephone, they called their folks. Usually their conversations were short and to the point. They would relate their latest experiences, then they were ready to go back aboard. If their grandmother baked, they helped. They discovered that their grandmother bakes the best home made bread and cinnamon rolls they ever tasted. She never makes these at home because the two of us would gain way to much weight.

One day the boys and I made a batch of fudge. It turned out very well, but they were surprised at being able to have as much as they wanted. Because of this freedom, they made the fudge last longer than I expected. We have a storage area next to the skin of the boat where we keep cans of soda pop as they keep cold here without refrigeration. The boys knew they could have a soda anytime they wanted, but they didn't abuse this privilege either.

At first we thought we would have to entertain the boys while they were with us on our small sailboat. "ITCHY FEET" is a Catalina 30. As it turned out there was little need for us to come up with something for them to do. They easily entertained themselves.

We were up early to catch the ebb tide, dropped our present mooring, got canvas up, and headed for Kingston, Washington. Once clear of lands end, I turned the helm over to Robbert. We were running down wind on a broad reach, an easy sail, but still requiring attention from the helmsman. I beamed with pride as I watched the boy feeling the vessel under his bare feet. He reminded me of Sterling Hayden and other old sailing masters of the past, men whose time seemed to have passed too soon for this youngster to have joined their ranks.

When the wind started picking up over an hour later, I asked Robbert, "She's kind'a movin fast isn't she?"

Unconcerned he replied. “Yep.” Still feeling very much in control.

I said. “Look aft and tell me what you see.”

Robbert turned, looked, and turned back at me. “What am I supposed to see grandpa?”

“The dark clouds aft. This wind you’re starting to feel is in front of a rain storm, an your carryin to much sail.”

We got the main down and ran on under the jib alone, still making five knots or better. We beat the rain into Kingston, but not by much.

Randal, my computer expert didn’t find the same pleasure from sailing as Robbert, but enjoyed other activities aboard. He was often at the helm, but his enthusiasm was different. Both boys seemed to have a natural feel for being in control, and making the boat behave the way it should. Something many adults have trouble with at first.

This Summer we will take Aireanna. She willingly pointed out to us that she is nine this year, and should be able to go on the boat. A young girl on board won’t be that much different. She’ll probably take a doll or two, plus some other toys she likes. I’m also sure her grandmother will see to it that they go shopping as well. She too, will have a log book and a work book, but I probably won’t have the same kind of input to her that her grandmother will have.

Sometimes I'm sure we do this for the grandchildren so they will have those old memories as they grow older. Other times I'm sure we do it so we will have those memories to share with others as we grow older.

THE B.E.D. SYNDROME

We were invited to a younger couple's home for dinner. They were aware of our latest cruise and, as wanna'be cruisers, they wanted to hear all about our travels. Lyn was okay with this arrangement, but I was fearful that my dreaded B.E.D. syndrome would overtake me without warning.

A few days later found us at their home during the early evening hours, and it happened during dinner. The trouble started like it most often does. Lyn, or myself would forget our surroundings while dining. I'd forget to use a fork while eating and would use a spoon instead. I prefer a large spoon when I can find one, but they are rare on a dining table. I'd never pick up a fork. And a knife would just be a waste of time, it has to be a spoon.

Sometimes I get lucky and Lyn remembers at the last second, Then she'll quickly reaching over under the table to gently touch my leg. Lyn tries to catch me before I start to lift a bowl up to my mouth to slurp the last of some food remnant, or juices out of whatever food container I'm using. On board our boat, using plates is unheard of, bowls are the only way to go.

Often while eating out with others, one of us will suddenly notice our hosts watching us with eyes that bordered on contempt, or least amazement. The realization that we were being watched again often spurred one, or both of us into action without thinking. one of us would say to whomever we were dining with, and looking at us, "*Sorry. It's the*

B.E.D. thing." After a few times, while dinning out, I discovered that folks thought we were spelling "bed," but we weren't.

Often when one of us would say the name of the syndrome one letter at a time, and that's really the only way to say it, I'd see a glint in the man's eyes, and a look of surprise on the woman's face. Surprise, that a man my age would still chase my sweety around the boat. This too, finally sank into my head, and it dawned on me of what they were thinking we'd meant. The man would think We were getting a lot of sack time in, heh, heh, heh. The woman would too, but the woman would think I was just an over sexed older man. Then Lyn, or I would have to go into the lengthy explanation mode.

A lot of people don't understand the B.E.D. syndrome. It's not easy to overcome. It starts easy enough though. So easy in fact that you don't even think about it. You become so used to eating off a table at home that you expect to eat the same way on board a boat when it's underway. You don't.

When you first begin to travel on a boat, you find that sometimes the best time of day, to start the daily trip, is to start out early. Like at the crack of dawn when the weather is still quiet.

To do this you often have to forgive the habit of eating at a dining table. You learn to eat as you can while you're underway.

I recall the first time this “Boat Eating Disorder” started. Lyn and I had left our marina early, as we’d scheduled a long day’s trip the first day out. Being the good wife she is she fixed me some bacon and scrambled eggs for breakfast, plus a cup of hot chocolate. She then brought it topside for me while I kept an eye out for other boating, or ship traffic. I put the boat on autopilot and sat down on the Starboard seat, sat my cup down near me, and started to eat my breakfast with a fork.

My boat doesn’t have a cockpit table, so I needed to hold my plate in my other hand. I held it because there just wasn’t any place nearby to set it down and still reach it to take a bite of breakfast and still see what was going on around me. The knife was just sliding all over the place so I stuck it in between the seat and a storage locker. With the knife out of the way, I could at least omit it from my mind.

I didn’t even notice the way my hand would automatically slant the plate from one angle to another in compensating for the occasional cross swell we’d encounter. That is until a very large power boat sent its wake in our direction.

When that happened I just made a grab for my cup of hot chocolate before the large curling wake got to us. Still, in my haste, some chocolate spilled out over the lip of the cup onto my pants leg.

"Whoooeee. hot." I'd said loud enough for Lyn to hear. After hearing the commotion she came to my rescue with a few paper towels to soak up the remnants of hot chocolate that had landed near my feet. Then, the white seat I'd been inhabiting was cleaned, and finally the engine control panel. When she found the knife stuck in the slot between the seat, and the storage locker, she took the knife below with her.

After the large wake passed us by I was still holding onto a plate half full of food. The fork was gone, I never did find it. I think it just jumped up off my plate and flew through the air going overboard. I think this happened when I'd jumped trying to out run the hot chocolate coming in my direction from a cup I was still holding onto.

Lyn had almost suffered the same fate. She'd been sitting at our table down below trying to eat her breakfast when the big wake had hit. She told me later that her breakfast had actually jumped off her plate and landed on the far side of the table. Well you get the picture.

Okay enough of that, let me explain how B.E.D. comes about. What happens is this. Over a period of time you change your eating habits while you travel. In fact they can become boat eating habits. Or "B" for boat, "E" for Eating, "D" for disorder.

You ask most anyone how they eat while underway and lots of them will tell you it's out of a bowl with a large spoon. For those of you who have yet to encounter eating this way, yet you want to travel, here's the scoop. You use a bowl for your meal, a large one most of the time, one of those deep kind of bowls. Plus a large spoon. Unless you have lots of experience with forks while underway a spoon is your better bet.

Because a fork can rarely cut anything well on the inside of a large bowl, a large spoon works much better. Knives just get left in the drawer, and only get used for opening your mail when you're able to get it. Yes, yes I hear you. Yes your food does get mixed together. Get used to it.

The long term affect of *B.E.D.* is that when you rejoin others of the non-traveling world, you forget how to eat their way. Then when you sit down to a meal, as we did with new fiends this evening, they look at you strangely. It's when you realize during the meal that you're holding your plate up in your hands near your face, while you're looking for your large spoon that you can't seem to find, that you catch them staring at you. After a while you just become used to explaining you suffer from a boat eating disorder.

It took me nearly a year before I remembered that, as we sat down to eat, I'd have to tell our hosts of our disorder. Even therapy for this illness takes awhile to kick in. Especially when your shrink is a boater.

A HOLE IN THE SAND

It had been late in the day when Lyn and I approached the area we had chosen to anchor. We normally anchored across the bay to the east, at Canoe Point, but we had arrived late and the area had been crowded when we arrived. It was then, that we decided to cross the Bay and try the west side for a change.

Motoring slowly we observed a large fishing boat anchored dead ahead, so we changed course to an area just to the north of the other vessle. As it began to shallow, we were about to turn back, when suddenly it got deeper. The water depth of some twenty plus feet looked good, so we dropped our anchor and set it firmly. As the tide was full, but in the stages of turning, the slight current pulled us to the east of our anchor.

We had gone to bed when it got dark and at sunrise we woke. It seemed strangely quiet as I climbed out of the Vee birth, quiet like it is when it has snowed. I headed aft to the galley to put water on for a cup of tea, and happened to look out of our open hatch to the south. The fishing boat, that had been anchored there, was gone. So was the water.

Befuddled I went topside, and to my amazement we were afloat in a large salt water puddle. The bay was now some two or three hundred feet east of us.

I went below to get my shorts, and said, "I have to go ashore."

Lyn said, "Like that?"

"No biggie, come have a look." Then I went aft, placed our extra anchor into the dink, and rowed but a short distance to set it in the sand astern of 'Endless Summer.' Now there was no worry about drifting to one side or the other of our puddle, it was only a matter of waiting for the tide to come back in, and of course hope it would be deep enough to allow us to escape to deeper water.

Lyn was standing in the cockpit looking good, nude, and commenting about being stuck in a hole in the sand. For some reason we had stayed right in this hole while the bay emptied around us, and the offshore breeze had kept us in the center. If it had not been for this set of circumstances, we would be scrubbing the bottom about now trying to look as though we had planned to be here for that very purpose.

As the remainder of the morning passed, we watched a few crabs walking around under the boat, and one starfish moving slowly about as well. It had been a good idea to set the stern anchor out, because as the tide returned it would have swept us into the sandy mud off our bow. In the long run, we had only to pull the boat aft while letting out slack on the bow anchor.

When we were over the stern hook it came up easily, and we swung gently forward over the other anchor. It too came up without hesitation.

The following night found us anchored in the lee of Canoe point, and we watched a small power boat head across the bay toward the other shoreline. We hoped he'd be lucky enough to anchor in the puddle.

LIVE-A-BOARDS

It was one of those balmy Saturday afternoons, and Lyn and I were sitting in the cockpit of our boat Endless Summer, and in the shade of our boom tent. The marina was busy with people doing boat chores, and in reality just messing around.

We hadn't been in this marina long, but we had gotten to know most of the other boaters in the nearby slips, and one of those couples, two slips south of us, was in the process of moving aboard. Lyn and I had moved aboard the winter before, so we understood the problems they would be encountering. When Bill and Helen appeared to have a few slack moments, I invited them over for a glass of wine, they accepted, and were sitting with us in a matter of moments.

Lyn and I were living aboard our Cascade 29 at that moment in time so we could understand the lack of storage space. Helen, on the other hand, held a position of power with the Port authority, and she had to dress the part. This meant she needed to maintain a fair wardrobe. Also, as she was new to living aboard, she was in a quandary as to where all of her clothing and makeup were going to be kept, and every boater knows hanging lockers are not very roomy.

The four of us chatted for about thirty minutes with most of the discussion centered around Helen's lack of storage on their boat, a thirty five footer.

Lyn and I had heard enough, but we were not about to say, "okay, enough already."

About this time another young couple passed by our stern in their dinghy. As they rowed by, they greeted us with an "Afternoon skipper." A common greeting, and continued on their way up the bay. A few minutes later they reappeared, and as they did so I said. "Why don't you two tie off to the dock and join us."

Nearly before the words finished coming out of my mouth, Jim and Jami wrapped their dinks bow line around a dock cleat, and the two of them climbed into our cockpit, and found a place to sit. After I poured them each a glass of wine the talk resumed, and Helen began explaining how little room she had on her small thirty-five foot boat for storage.

After a few minutes, I asked, "So. . . Jim, I've seen you two around here often."

"Yes, we live aboard about two docks over." his fingers pointing to the east.

Helen, couldn't leave well enough alone, she asked, "Well, how big is the boat you live on?"

Jami said. "Twenty-four feet."

Helen never again brought up how little storage she had to contend with during the conversation.

HEADING SOUTH, AND CAN'T READ A CHART

Lyn and I had anchored in Grandma's Cove. A small anchorage area just off the Columbia River, and downstream from the railroad bridge and the Interstate highway five. On the day after our arrival, another sailboat came in and anchored just to the north of us. A young couple with two children on board. Lyn and I always welcome other boaters aboard our vessel, so the invitation was offered to our new neighbors, and they accepted.

When they came aboard "Endless Summer," we gave the children a can of soda pop, while we adults shared a glass of wine and told boating stories. We asked if they had been down river to a popular spot called, 'The Pond.' They had not, and asked if we might come aboard their boat that same evening and show them where it is located on their chart.

Later in the day we were welcomed aboard their nice thirty eight foot boat, shown below, and given something to sip as we gave them instructions on how to get to, and enter the Pond. Ben placed a brand new chart on the table, and I showed him the spot just below St.Helens Oregon.

As I explained, "You'll need to favor the Washington side of the slough when you go in, as it shallows right here by this marker."

"Okay, so go over here on this side?" He said, tracing a route with his finger.

"Yes, then after you round this corner here, and as you are preparing to go in through this small cut, stay in the center of the channel, especially at low tide."

His wife, Marilyn, who had been looking over our shoulders, said. "What are all those little round circles there?"

She was pointing to the nautical chart's placement of old pilings and I thought, "Well perhaps she doesn't know that much about navigation, but she should learn. "Those are pilings. You know, those posts that they tie log booms up to?"

"Oh, sure."

Then Ben said, "What are all these numbers all over the paper for?"

Now, I was very surprised and concerned. "That is the depth of the water, and your chart will tell you up here in the corner what the depth is," my fingers pointing to the fathom notation.

It was a few weeks further into the summer, when a mutual friend of ours told me, "Ben and Marilyn are heading south."

"Did he learn anything about navigation?" I asked.

"You mean he doesn't know how to navigate?"

"Not the last time I talked with him he didn't."

One afternoon later in the year, and as I was walking on a nearby dock, I came across a little girl I recognized, heading further down an adjacent walkway. I said to her, “I thought you and your folks were going south on your boat?”

“Uhuh, we did.”

“Oh. Well you didn’t stay very long huh?”

“No. See we gots in this giant storm when we were out in the Ocean, and me’n mommy got sick.”

“That happens sometimes,” I answered.

“Well it was scary, bad scary. Then mommy and daddy talked about things, and mommy and me and Jimmy gots on an airplane in California and camed home again.”

“And what happened to daddy?” I’m knew it was none of my business and these things happen to the best of us, but you know how curiosity is.

“Daddy stayed down there awhile, thens he gots a truck to bring our boat back up here.”

This is a true story, yet it is a common thing for those unknowing, to just take off for far away places, trusting in following con trails from over flying jet aircraft to lead them to Hawaii, or other places. This couple figured they would just follow the coastline south until they got to their desired location.

PRAIRIE CHANNEL & THE NAVY

While Portland Oregon was celebrating Rose Festival, Lyn and I had spent the entire week naked, though at the time we were in total isolation on the mighty Columbia River.

Prairie channel is a remote section of the lower Columbia River, just above Astoria. It is located a very short distance northeast of the old Naval shipyards and easterly from Tongue Point. In the more recent history, the area was been used for log storage in the form of log rafts. We had in fact, spent the week moored to one of these log rafts.

Now however, as the visiting Naval ships berthed in Portland for Rose Festival, a traditional event, and were preparing to depart for the open sea, we too were preparing to return to Oregon Slough where we lived on our houseboat. With our short vacation coming to an end, we had to return to the hectic life of the big city.

Our morning started bright, sunny, and very warm. Because of the warmth Lyn and I took the option of sailing home in the nude. Well, nearly all the way home. We planned on putting some clothes on once we got into heavier boat traffic further upriver. Until then we would enjoy the feel of mother nature surrounding us.

We cast our lines loose from the log raft, and turned south. We wanted to get to the open waters of the Columbia river in the shortest time and distance available. We could have gone north up a backwater slough, and joined the Columbia to the northeast, but this would have taken much longer due to the careful navigation this route demands.

Once we cleared Tongue Point, we turned up-river. On our new course we raised our jib, and the mainsail, as it would be a comfortable downwind run, but upstream. The air off the Pacific ocean filling Astoria bay, was also on its way up the Columbia River Gorge, and ultimately the inland plains. This meant we could probably run downwind the entire trip home.

We settled into a Port beam reach, knowing that when we rounded Miller Sands, our trip upriver would be a continual downwind run. Lyn had taken the helm, and sat on the high side of the cockpit facing east taking in the sun. It warmed her, and she looked beautiful in her natural state. Her back, turned toward the major portion of the river allowed her to keep an eye on our position in regards to the eastern shoreline.

An occasional glance forward helped her maintain her compass direction by checking her drift with the currents, and watching for the next marker buoy just ahead. The depth sounder was near her left shoulder for an update when she needed it for reference as to the depth of the water presently under our keel. We had sailed this river many times and know it pretty well so there was no reason to worry.

When we had settled into a routine, I, in turn, went below to fix us something to sip on. Perhaps supply us with something to munch on as well. As I started below, I looked upstream and in the distance I could see a naval vessel coming downstream, obviously heading out to sea from Portland. I thought nothing of it, as it was on the far side of the river, and in the deepest part of the channel.

As it turned out, I had just finished getting our drinks and snacks together when I heard a loudspeaker. "All hands, eyes to Port." I had never considered the fact that Yes, the navy does keep lookouts with binoculars scanning the horizon for anything that might concern a ship's navigation even in rivers. In this case it was a nude woman sailing a boat, and apparently by herself.

Lyn, without thinking turned to see where the noise had come from and raised up to get a better view. The sailors, on board the ship, now had a nearly full frontal view of a very pleasing nude woman at the helm of a sloop passing them by to Port.

Her words of "Oh my God" were quite audible to me still below decks in the main cabin.

I smiled as I said. "Not to worry sweetheart. They'll never see you again. But, you will undoubtedly be mentioned in the ship's log."

Both the naval ship, and the sailboat continued on their previously determined course. After this encounter, and while Lyn was on the helm, if a ship was going to pass us going outbound I was immediately notified, “Your turn to sail.”

After the ship passed by, our female Captain would return to the cockpit, again resuming command.

COLUMBIA RIVER BAR, VS JUAN DE FUCA

The Columbia River bar leading into Astoria Oregon, and the far reaches of the inland Columbia River waterways, has a fierce reputation. Shipwrecks litter the sea bottom in this section of the Oregon coastline. Even inside the bay there are wrecks strung along the sandbars, some are still being found yet today and the remnants of one, the Peter Iredale, can still be seen poking its rusting hulk up out of the sandy surf.

These are not Spanish Galleon carrying rich cargo's of gold, these are ships that may have been carrying goods to trade the Indian tribes for pelts which would have been worth gold had they ever arrived back in their home ports. Many carried cargo's of logs bound for sawmills, such as those found in San Francisco California in those years.

There are ship's hulls strung along the coastline for miles north and south of this famed river bar of danger, yet little is said about a more dangerous bar to the north. Not really a bar per se, but an entrance to a large waterway non-the-less.

The entrance into the Puget Sound area, not far from Seattle Washington, the San Juan Islands, and Channel Islands of British Columbia, has a water flow in and out of Juan De Fuca Straight that is unbelievable. The length of Puget Sound is such that as the tide begins to flow back into the opening of Juan De Fuca, it is still ebbing at the other end. The only area that can even come close to this is the opening into San Francisco Bay to the south. Ask any skipper where the 'Potato Patch' is located and he'll tell you, "It's just outside of the 'Golden Gate.'

But the story about the great waterway leading into Puget Sound goes untold. When a small boat enters, or leaves this waterway, it is not unusual to have wave heights that block out any view in any direction during the transit. Having sailed a thirty foot boat through this wide opening of Juan De Fuca, there are times I swear the waves were above the top of the mast, and this is during fair weather. If memory serves me, I believe the width at the opening is about seventeen miles across.

This, is a transit that has found many a commercial vessel in trouble, and there is, at the time, a large tugboat at the ready in nearby Neah Bay to assist ships in distress as they enter the Straights.

GOOD TIMES ABOUND

In San Francisco, California 1974 in Ayala Cove, Angel Island, 1400 hours plus or minus. The small marine park buoys were nearly filled to capacity. There were two or three buoys on the South Western side open, but that was all. The tide was flooding which left the small bay with a tidal water movement circling clockwise.

Most boaters were in and set for the day or longer, and as was the custom, on arriving you're expected to pick up a bow and stern buoy. This allows more usable space for the many boats that seek anchorage in this small, and very popular marine park.

Those who get in early, watch the late arrivals as a form of afternoon or evening entertainment. This incident happened about mid afternoon. As onlookers watched this afternoon, a 28' to 30' powerboat entered the bay on the north east side.

The skipper motored slowly around the outer perimeter of the bay, apparently seeking an empty and available set of buoys. The skipper was sitting at the helm on the fly bridge, looking very macho. The woman aboard, in a very relaxed manner, sat on the other chair on the fly bridge.

Busily, he manipulated the engine throttles, and the transmissions shifting levers. She, very much kicked back, was filing her fingernails. When He had the boat situated between two of the remaining buoys, he put the boat's engines in neutral and quickly rose from his captains chair, then hurried down the ladder, just aft of the fly bridge, to the lower deck.

Arriving at the bow, he caught the mooring buoy with his Boat hook and made short work of tying the bow line off to the buoy. Because park rules stipulate a boat needs to be tied off bow and stern, he rushed aft for his stern line. This attempt proved fruitless as the buoy was by now out of reach.

She meanwhile, still sat doing her nails on the fly bridge apparently unconcerned. He now seemed to be in more of a hurry. He quicken his pace up the ladder to the fly bridge, sat in the Captain's chair, put the engines in reverse gear, and again backed the boat up to the stern buoy. A little quicker now he nearly slid down the ladder, and with a quickened step walked aft to pick up the stern buoy, only to find it was already out of reach. The tide was pulling him away from it between the time he backed the boat up, and made his way to the stern.

This time while heading toward the fly bridge, he skipped some steps on the ladder. Once more at the controls, the engines were engaged in reverse gear, and the boat moved back to the mooring buoy with a little more gusto. By the time he retraced his path to the stern, the buoy was again out of reach. However, this time he discovered he also needed more slack in his bow line.

She, still filing her nails and quite relaxed in her chair, seemed oblivious to his efforts. He ran to the bow, let some line out on his bow line, ran aft to the ladder leading to the fly bridge. Now his footing only found every third rung as he raced to the controls, and began backing the boat up once again.

She now appeared to be applying polish to her nails, bright red perhaps. On this trip while descending the ladder his feet barely touched the rungs, his hands slipping on the rails, as a fireman might do while descending the pole to the fire truck in preparation of going to a fire. She was now working on the other hand.

He ran aft, jumping over some item on his cockpit floor, a boat pole in hand, desperately reaching out for, and finally getting a hold on the stern mooring buoy. You could hear a round of applause throughout the marine park. Though, she was still working on her finger nails at this point, things quieted down on the boat, some what.

He walked casually forward, climbed the ladder one step at a time, shut the engines down. His heart rate must have been soaring. Within a few minutes the two of them had gone down the ladder, and inside the main salon, the curtains were drawn.

About forty minutes later, he was back on the fly bridge, the engines were started, and the curtains were now open. The bow and stern lines were cast off, and they slowly motored out of the park.

She, once more working on her nails.

A FORMAL DINNER

Boaters, for the most part, are a gregarious bunch of people. After spending so much time alone those on cruising boats often seek the company of others when they anchor in locations where cruisers are found lying to a hook. Once anchored, it only takes a short time before someone from another boat arrives in their dinghy. After introductions, an invitation usually follows to join a group for a get-together aboard one boat or another.

Every boater understands the un-written rules of getting together with others in these situations, each boating family brings something to the gathering. Land lubber's would call them pot luck dinners. On boats, they are more understood as story times with food.

Because of this way of thinking, Lyn and I nearly made a mistake in our life ashore after we first swallowed the hook. We decided to have a few new friends over for a dinner in our shore home, nothing fancy, you know a boater's dinner. Well, it was to be that kind of dinner in our minds, that is until one of our invited guests called Lyn and asked, "Lyn, thank you for the invitation to dinner. I'm calling because I make a lovely dessert, and I can bring some for the other guests to share if you like."

Lyn thanked her and said, "Of course you can."

I could only hear half of the conversation, but I was proud of her, this was one of the few times she remembered she didn't have to say, "Over" as if talking on the radio. I suppose it was because she only had to put the phone down, instead of hanging the VHF mike on a hook near the radio.

After putting the phone down, she sat in silence, only her hands seemed fidgety, until I asked, "What's up Babe?"

She looked at me with a blank expression, the one you see on a new computer user's face when they don't know which way to move the mouse, or when to double click the left or right mouse button.

Then she said, "These are not boaters coming to dinner."

"I know," I said as calmly as I could, but I was becoming concerned because she said it to me in such a manner that it was supposed to reveal something, and my mind was coming up empty. You know, like when you see a big wave breaking at your stern, and knowing their isn't a damn thing you can do but ride it out, and hope you stay dry.

"Well, she continued, this means I have to fix a complete dinner. You know, from scratch."

Oh-oh, now the picture was becoming clear to me. Lyn and I had been cruising for nine years give or take, and when you spend that much time on a boat, one pot meals become a way of life. This is done to second guess mother nature's whims concerning the weather. No matter what mother nature decides, you have a meal easily prepared for eating while underway. Of course many of these meals are eaten with a big spoon, and from the confines of a large bowl.

I tried to respond correctly. "Well, do you want'a go to a Deli and have something fixed, orrrr . . . ?" Okay, I was a little heavy on the 'Or' part, because I could picture the cost of a gallon of good bottom paint going to hell. Perhaps that's not the right word, but you get the idea.

"No, no no noo. Can't do that, I've just got to actually cook a meal, a real meal."

I was glad to hear this, but I wasn't sure I could eat a meal that consisted of more than one course. Then, I had a revelation, "Sweety, why don't you fix several different boat meals?"

She looked at me with wonderment in her eyes, like I'd just made my first wire to rope splice. "That's a perfect solution."

The morning of our 'Dinner Party', she was busier than a new deck hand hauling in their first anchor. She was cooking all sorts of things, making little snack things that I only vaguely remembered from times before cruising.

I, on the other hand, was reviewing my sea stories, you know the ones about storms, and such. Of course, I was sampling some of our better wines, the ones I'd chosen for our evening meal. Yes, the ones that cost more than four or five bucks a bottle, and yes, the smaller bottles, not the six dollar, five liter bottles.

Our guests arrived as planned, and the eight of us sipped a little wine. I'd forgotten how some of these shore folks like to drink. Three bottles later, we sat at the table to dine, and of course to drink more wine.

Lyn, had fixed eight of my favorite boat meals, so it was a success to me right off the bat. To everyone else it was just an exquisite eight course meal. I say exquisite, because our guests had never experienced these kinds of dishes, and they thought Lyn was outstanding in her delightful culinary masterpieces.

I thought it was exquisite because we used plates, and had the whole selection of knives, forks, and spoons. Even the glasses we drank wine in were those fancy kind, you know, like the ones you used to have before you moved aboard your boat. Sure, those with ah, ah. . . stems, oh sure stemware.

Our guests seemed to forgive my lack of serving white or red wine, depending upon the course of the meal. Though, it could have been the fact that they may not have known which wine went with each different serving. Or, it may have been the fact they were pretty well liquored up.

Lyn had wowed ‘em with her great meal, and after we retired, catch that ‘retired’ . . . to the living room, I began to tell some of my more memorable sea stories. Some of them would start simply as, “Now this is a true story.”

FROZEN IN THE ICE.

When we woke up one morning, the boat seemed odd. As if we were hard aground, we weren't, but that's how it felt. Curiosity caused me to pull our main hatch open, and I found the marina was completely frozen over, we were stuck in solid ice. Never mind the snow that covered everything.

This was our first winter to explore in the North-West, as Lyn and I had come up the coast from the Columbia River in Oregon. When we arrived in Puget Sound, we spent only enough time to replenish the boat in Port Townsend, then we headed north into Canadian waters. We spent three months gunkholing in areas that lets the mind wander back a hundred years. The areas we visited were so pristine and so isolated, it was easy to feel as if you were the only humans around.

Like the trip into an area called 'Chatter Box falls.' This is a forty mile trip into very rugged country. Sheer rock walls surround you en route, trees barely taking root on sheer rock walls, or growing out of rocky outcropping, then bending upward toward the sky. In the spring, you can pass sixty five waterfalls on the way toward the far end of this dog legged group of Fjords. Eagles are common as they swoop down for fresh fish hiding just below the water's surface, Orcas passing by the boat while hunting for their own meal.

When our Canadian entry clearance permit expired, we decided to spend the winter in Everett Washington. This marina is located up the Snohomish river, and only a breakwater separates the river and marina from the salt water sound. Luckily, we found a slip we could sublease for the winter months at the back of the marina. This turned out well, as there was little boating traffic this far back in the basin.

By the time winter set in, we were both working at temporary positions, which would build up our cruising fund for the following summer's cruising. We brought our car up from the Oregon storage yard for our use, and we planned on putting it in storage somewhere nearby for the coming summer months.

Winter just seemed to happen overnight. One day the weather was nice, the next day it began to snow. Seems the Snohomish river water flows over the top of the salt water in the marina, to a depth of about four inches, and that, is what froze.

During the time the marina was frozen, several people just walked across the thick ice, ultimately taking a short cut from their boats to the gate at the head of the walkway. Footprints could be seen going in every direction.

Everett Washington marina is one of the largest in Puget sound, and it is very well maintained. However the waiting list for permanent moorage is long, but you can find notices on the various bulletin boards for boat slips available to sublease. We found you can sublease year round. Of course you may have to move from one slip to another on occasion.

WRITING ABOARD

For writers who are living aboard their boats, you already understand how great this living environment is for writing. For those who are not familiar with this lifestyle, there are many benefits, and there are pitfalls.

A few of the benefits include the quiet seclusion, being away from the daily phone calls, you merely unplug these when you are away from the dock, or traveling. Though, there can be radio telephone calls. However, these kinds of calls are easier to ignore than that of a ringing telephone. If you have a cellular telephone you may need to turn it off. You can explain you do this to save the battery for when it may really be needed. There won't be a newspaper delivered to your door, yet in many marinas, this can be arranged.

Your family will not be dropping in un-announced, mostly because they never know if you will be in a marina, or out on the water or anchored somewhere, writing of course. They will want you to keep in touch, because they may want to take you out to dinner just to be sure, you're eating correctly. Your children may expect to go boating with you when you'd really rather write something. However, grandchildren are another story. You'll take them boating anytime because they are a source of story material, and they are fun.

Your mind has the time to wander freely, to explore any number of realms you desire. The thought process will not be hampered by unexpected interference, and you may find that this kind of seclusion can bring out the creative writer easily. You may start to write with the intention of only writing for an hour or so, only to find the day has disappeared.

You can write in the warmth of the cabin on cold, rainy, and windy days. Or, you may find yourself out in the cockpit, with a pen and paper, a laptop computer, or a small portable word processor on those warm sunny days. Perhaps a glass of wine within reach, a few snacks to munch on, and the words flowing onto the page before you.

If you tire of writing, or just need a break from the keyboard, it is a simple matter of lying back and letting your eyelids slam shut for a few Zeee's. The freshness of a short nap will bring forth renewed vigor, and words can again appear with ease.

Well sure, it isn't always this nice. If, you are raising a family aboard, your writing time will suffer greatly, but it will be available if you work at obtaining the time.

Your editor may have trouble reaching you, unless you make arrangements for scheduled radio telephone calls as needed. If, your editor expects material from you on a timely basis, spell and grammar checked, double spaced, with an SASE, and the correct amount of words, it is easily arranged.

You probably won't know what's going on in the world, because you don't get a newspaper, you may not watch television, though you can if you really want to watch the world you are holding at bay.

You might find a ready market in the boating world magazines for 'How-to' articles, boating travel articles, or interesting feature stories. You may also find markets in a few travel magazines, or local newspapers. Though newspapers are not known for paying writers for freelance work, it can be good for the writer's ego, and producing publishing clips for your writer's resume.

Of course there is always the book world to consider, and if this is your aim you must remember that most books do not just fall together, they can take from two to four years to complete. No, this is not just sitting down to write, it is a matter of writing, then re-writing, and self editing. Yes the grammar, the punctuation, all of the stuff you hated in school.

When this is done, you need to find an publisher. "Oh," you say, "I'll just get an agent."

Well this is like getting your first job. You needed the job to get the experience, and you needed the experience to get the job. In the case of an agent, you almost need to be published to get an agent to help you become published.

Writing is hard work, but it is fun, and very rewarding to the one penning the words for others to read, and reading is like vitamins for the mind.

What to do about writing equipment can become a problem unless you plan ahead with a clear path to follow. I can tell you how I do my writing aboard. Perhaps this will give you some ideas on how to arrange your own methods.

I keep a complete computer system aboard my boat, computer, mouse, keyboard, printer, and a scanner. I also keep a good old fashioned typewriter aboard. I found a good one at a 'Goodwill' store, and one that felt comfortable to me, and that worked easily. I also keep some of that gooyey white out stuff around just in case. Going back to a typewriter keyboard from a computer keyboard seems weird, and tiring, but when you need the words to flow any keyboard will do. However, my real gem is a small word processor produced by 'AlphaSmart Inc.'at www.smartinput.com, this portable unit runs on three double A batteries, which seem to last forever.

Mine will hold about a hundred pages of information, but I think the newer machines will hold even more, and, also have much more magic available for the user, even my older one has more abilities than I take advantage of. When out away from shorepower, and my computer cannot be used, I use the smaller AlphaSmart. Then when I get to a power source, I plug my AlphaSmart into a USB port on the computer with the cable provided by the same company, and simply push the 'Send' key which downloads all of my latest writing into my normal word processor.

RUM RUNNERS

It was late afternoon when Lyn and I picked up a Provincial park buoy under sail in Bedwell harbour of South Pender Island. We planned on being here for the night, maybe two if needed. We were not trying to show off by picking up the buoy under sail, we had too. Yet, we still arrived in time to be visited by the local Canadian park ranger, he was expecting the mooring fees for the buoy. The Canadian fees are reasonable, and the rangers are very friendly, friendly enough for me to ask for help.

While we were chatting, I mentioned we needed a set of spark plugs for our sick Atomic four engine, as it was nearly impossible to start, and the winds had been very fickle the last couple of days. Normally I wouldn't be too concerned, but we were going to cross over Boundry Pass, then enter Haro strait. Both of which can become very nasty, but ultimately lead to Roche Harbor and the ability to clear customs back into the United States. I wanted to be able to use the engine if we needed it to stay out of trouble during our transit of these waterways.

He mentioned to me that a friend of his was going over to Roche Harbor in the morning, and he'd have him come by to pick me up and give me a ride over, if that would work for us. I assured him I would be grateful for the ride.

As it turned out his friend Jacque, was later arriving at our boat than expected, and he was in a hurry. Not wanting to hold him up I grabbed my money clip, shoved it into my empty pocket, and kissed my wife goodbye.

I was impressed with the boat Jacque had as I climbed aboard. There was no question, this thing was fast. It was so fast it was nearly on its steps and skimming across the open bay before I sat down on a seat adjacent seat to the young skipper.

In would have taken me a much longer time to cross the open waterways, this boat delivered the two of us to Roche harbor in a very short time. The ride across was, shall we say, exhilarating. I don't think I've ever traveled this fast, well maybe in an airplane. I suppose if you are used to riding in extremely fast boats, it may not have meant a thing, but to a rag sailor, it was definitely impressive.

When we entered Roche harbor, on the western side of Pearl Island, Jacque didn't even bother to slow down. In fact we were well into the crowd of boats near the fuel dock before his boat began to lose way.

He tied her off far inside of the fuel dock area, just below the Post Office, and was up and out of the boat before I got some stability back into my legs again.

"Back soon mate," he said, and was gone. He hadn't bothered clearing customs coming in, he just tied up as if he lived here.

I'd rounded up my spark plugs and was sitting at an outdoor table overlooking the marina, and watching a fellow in uniform looking at the power boat I'd arrived on. I thought he was just admiring the boat, so I did not worry. He seemed to hang around for a while, then he left.

It was sometime later when Jacque returned, and he and I hastily clambered aboard. Quickly the engines came to life, and we were off. He cranked up the power while still in the main marina basin, and horns were tooting from every boat, and from every direction. Yes, yes, this is a no wake zone. The fines can be extensive depending on the situations.

We were leaving Roche Harbor the same way we came in, by going out past Pearl Island. Just as we were exiting the main bay I could see a patrol boat in the harbor heading our way at high speed, with lights flashing, and I could hear what sounded like a siren blaring. I said, "I think that guy want's to talk to you Jacque."

Jacque said, "Oh no. He's been after me for some time." When the Harbor patrol boat caught up to us Jacque stopped the boat.

As the patrol boat came along side, the uniformed officer expressed his heated opinion about the speed we had used in Roche harbor. Angrily he began to write a ticket for the flagrant speed and endangering the boats and people in the area of the fuel dock.

As the officer asked why our boat was going so fast, Jacque said, “Well, I’ve got a bag full of money in the bilge, and I didn’t want to get caught with it.”

The officer in the patrol boat, stopped writing, looked at Jacque, and said, “A bag full of money, why do you have a bag full of money?”

“It was to buy the cigarettes and whiskey also in the bilge, that I’m smuggling back into Canada.”

The officer began to untie his boat from ours, and said. “You stay where you are, just let her drift, don’t start your engines, or move about.” After cutting loose from us, he started his engine and began doing slow turns around us, and at the same time he was on his radio.

I was taken aback by what had just taken place, and me without any identification, only a few bucks in a money clip in my pocket, but Jacque didn’t seem the least bit concerned. It was only a short time before a border patrol boat came along side Jacque’s boat. Then after rafting to us, one officer said. “I understand you’re smuggling contraband back into Canadian waters?”

Jacque, acting very surprised, said, “What, who told you that kind of story?”

“The officer from the Roche Harbor patrol boat called us, and explained the situation concerning this boat. Do you deny what he’s told us?”

“I certainly do.”

“He also told us you have a bag full of money aboard.”

“That’s not true. Why would he tell you such a thing.”

Now mind you, this is coming out of the mouth of an innocent looking, young man, who barely looks as if he needs to shave. As if he’s playing with his grandfathers boat, and of course, I look like a grandfather.

“Well, if its not true, you won’t mind if I have a look around your boat.”

“Why of course not. Please come aboard.” With that, Jacque stepped back giving the boarding officer plenty of room. His partner all the while keeping a close suspicious eye on both of us.

During the officers very thorough search, Jacque kept up a dialog of constant disbelief about the absurdity of being accused of such a crime. Finally, when the search was finished and as the officer apologized for our inconvenience, and the apparent mistake. Jacque said. “I suppose he told you we were speeding too?”

WORKING WINTERS & PLAYING SUMMERS

We cured the empty nest syndrome by leaving home ourselves. We were still young enough to play, and health problems had not, as yet, begun to cause us any problems.

The saying among boaters is to go cruising when you are still young enough to do so. We weren't exactly spring chickens at the time, I myself being just over fifty years of age at that time, Lyn many years younger, and we seemed to be in very good health. At that age I still felt I was invincible, and that nothing could, or would harm me.

When Leanna, our youngest daughter left home, Lyn and I sold our houseboat on the Oregon Slough, and moved onto our sailboat, which at the time was "Endless Summer" a Cascade 29 built in Portland Oregon

With the children gone, we felt it was time for us to go play, and so began a nine year cruise. Though all of our cruising took place within six or seven hundred miles of our former home, and relatives, it was nine years of fun. For a change our children worried about us, ahh yes. . . turn about is fair play.

Don't confuse cruising with distances traveled, cruising is actually a state of mind. There are those boaters who, on a whim, think nothing of traveling several hundred miles across open water to visit some remote location.

The fact of the matter is that you can travel to remote locations, and be within a hundred or so miles from your point of departure.

Lyn and I found several locations that were so remote, yet so near to civilization, that if we saw another boat on a daily basis, we felt as if the area was crowded. Sometimes we might see two or three boats a day, then it really was crowded. Often we found ourselves in remote locations where few other boaters ever explored. Sometimes we found out that the reason the areas were deserted is because they were so dangerous. I suppose our curiosity to go gunkholing in the out of the way places is what led us into some of these areas. In those places we just travel very slow and very easy. In all of the locations we have traveled to, we were within easy reach of a small town or settlement of some kind.

The term, gunkholing comes from poking your boats bow into unknown nooks and crannies along waterways that are not well defined on your charts. Of course there is always a danger of going aground, or hitting something, so keep a sharp eye out and go slow.

The question in most wan'na cruiser's minds is, how can someone do this kind of cruising and still eat and maintain their vessel. Actually, it isn't as hard as you might think. You only need to find some method of bringing in an income during the time of year when you are not cruising.

Lyn and I stumbled upon a very nice situation to provide us with cruising funds for our summer cruising. Sometimes the winter's work would produce enough income to allow us to play the following year or maybe two.

Let me tell you how we spent our winters. We stayed in some of the choicest motels, or hotels on the coast. Always having very nice rooms, enjoying extremely pleasant company, taking walks on the beach pretty much when we wanted too, eating as we liked, and the toughest part of it was we were getting paid to be there. That's right, we got paid to do this.

How? you say. It was easy, we were relief managers. A relief manager is someone who takes over the business when the regular managers, or owners take their vacation, and normally this is in the winter months. We got started in this business by answering an advertisement in the newspaper. A motel was looking for relief managers for two to four days a month. We applied, and accepted for the position. Soon another motel a few miles up the coast heard about us, and asked if we could take care of their days off as well. In those nine years of cruising, we had fifteen motels we were baby sitting during the owners, or managers vacations. We worked when we wanted, charged them for the wages we wanted, and always kept the summer months for ourselves.

Let's face it, odds are you'll spend the winter months holed up someplace, so go to work while you are there. The secret is not to go looking for the high paying executive positions, look for jobs that others don't want to do, or come up with an unusual service to others that will fill your cruising fund account.

If You can locate a temporary employment agency near your wintering location, you might find a selection of positions that suit your personal needs readily available.

In reality there are always jobs open for house keepers in the hotel motel industry, jobs as dishwashers and waitresses at restaurants, etc. Of course you may not want to do these things, but, you're cruising remember, and those you work with will admire what it is you are doing. In most cases, you'll be setting a very good example for those who may be struggling just to survive. Your lifestyle is one of envy by everyone, wealthy, or poor.

Probably the hardest part any kind of cruising is the fact that often cruising and being materialistic do not go hand in hand. Most cruisers reach the point where they realize it may be necessary to give up owning homes, cars, sometimes insurance policies, anything that takes money out of the cruising fund each month.

How long can you do this, as long as you want. Lyn and I continued this life style until it dawned on us one spring, we were only going sailing on nice warm sunny days. We no longer sailed among ice floes, during snow storms, or rainy and terrible weather, only on nice days. Shortly after that we received an offer for our boat, that was timely and substantial, so we sold her.

Do we regret swallowing the hook, as they say, not really. Once in awhile we look at the open water near our present home, smile while remembering the wonderful years we enjoyed exploring. You may hear one of us giving a sigh, but living on the land is okay with us, we did what we wanted, and when we wanted. Now you take a turn, you'll not regret having done so.

When you wake up some morning to a warming sun, pick up a book and head topside to the cockpit, first thing you know it's time for a glass of wine, then just as suddenly it's beginning to get dark, the day is done. Tomorrow you have to do it all over again. Get dressed, naw, no need for that.

FISHING WITH DYNAMITE

As children, my brother Richard and I, often played on a river near our home in the summer months. And, as young boys often do, we built a raft out of wood found on the beach along our favored portion of the river. We kept our raft, and its poles, in a small cove, or backwater, perhaps thirty feet across, on the north side of the river, and just below a railroad trestle. It was the same railroad that we walked along to get to the river to the south of our home.

We always foraged for Anything we might use for our raft while making he trip to the river and we usually had a paper sack lunch in hand. But one morning we encountered an event that would bring back memories for the remainder of our lives. Richard and I, upon arriving at the trestle, looked under the bridge to see if there were any Hobos sleeping under there. Which did, on occasion take place. I don't recall our ever being afraid of any physical harm from Hobos, but we did give them a wide berth if they looked questionable.

On this day we did not see anyone under the bridge, but we did see a wooden box, and out of curiosity, we looked inside. Without hesitation we pulled the box of Dynamite out from under the bridge, a stamp on the side of the case listed the railroad's name, and, if I remember correctly, something telling about its being twenty percent.

Apparently, a work crew had stashed it there during the week, never expecting anyone to come across its contents.

Of course as children, we had no idea of the potential danger, to the two of us it was just big firecrackers. Some of the sticks had been cut into smaller pieces, and there was a box of matches, and fused caps in the box as well. We found one short piece with a fused cap pushed into the end, so we walked out onto the trestle and when we were nearly over the small backwater where our raft was tied to a tree, we lit the fuse and tossed the Dynamite down into the water below us.

The resulting explosion wasn't really loud, but the size of the geyser of water was a surprise to us. After things settled a bit, we saw fish rising to the surface of the water. We were not a wealthy family by any means, so from our raft Richard and I began collecting the dead fish.

We were able to carry several fish home in our paper bag, though we'd had to be careful because of the damp bottom. Once we got home, we found there was not enough room in our mom's refrigerator, so we had to get rid of some fish.

Being the good kids we were, we decided to give some fish to our neighbors. They were accepted as if Richard and I were master fishermen. This of course was part of our undoing, as young egos began to spark into flames, and even the fish we had intended to keep for our mom, were soon given away before she got home from work.

For the next two weeks, the neighbors welcomed the neighbor boys, Donald and Richard, when they came to the door with fresh fish. As we were latch key children, our mother never knew about our fishing forays. One day, in front of our home, we were greeted by a man, who said, “I hear you two boys are quite the fishermen?”

By now of course, we had pretty large heads, swelled with pride of course, and we replied. “Yep” almost in unison.

“Would you mind taking me fishing with you?”

As Dick and I saw no harm in that, we agreed. “Can you go now?” I asked.

“Sure.”

The three of us walked along the railroad track, and the friendly man kept asking questions. Some we answered, some we didn’t.

After we got to the river, Dick took the man down to our raft while I went to get one of our remaining short sticks of Dynamite. Though our raft was a little skittish with three of us, we poled out into the center of our small backwater bay, and I pulled the dynamite contents out of the inside of my shirt. Without thinking I might be doing something wrong, I lit the match and touched it to the fuse, then handed it to the man who was trying to keep his balance.

He had been telling us, in these last seconds, that he was with the state department of fish and game, and that killing fish with Dynamite was against the law. Now, however, he was holding a smoking fuse stuck in a short stick of danger.

I asked, “Are you gon’na fish or talk.”

I'M LOOKING FOR A CHARLIE NOBLE

We'd been in a squall on our approach to the Bay at San Francisco California, and while passing under the Golden Gate Bridge we jibed the rig, and not intentionally. Though we were under a double reefed main, the noise created by the sudden stop of the boom was inspiring not to do it again.

As the main boom came sweeping across the coach roof a short loop, from one of the reefing point lines, caught just under the top of our existing 'Charlie Noble.' In doing so, it ripped the top right off the stand pipe riser.

Well into the bay we found two adjacent buoys, at Angel Island, and tied off bow and stern, this method of mooring is required by this state park facility. The following morning I caught the ferry from Tiburon, and paid for a wrong way round trip ticket. Whereas, park visitors leave the mainland and come out to the island for the day, I was going from the island to the mainland for the day.

Eventually I found my way to Sausolito, a few short miles away, and my search for a Chandlery proved worthwhile, I was in search of a replacement stove pipe cap. I walked into the only Chandlery in the area, and found the store only had one employee working at the time. This surprised me as this is a large boating community. Inside, I began looking for a stainless steel stove pipe cap, and was not having any luck.

After a few minutes, a young man was able to tear himself away from a personal phone call, and came to my rescue. So he thought.

“Can I help you find something?”

“Yes. I’m looking for a Charlie Noble.” Though this is a name of a stove part, it is, and has been known by this name for decades. That is, to those in the boating world.

I could see his face contort some as he pondered my question. Finally, he came out with, “I don’t think he works here.”

SMUGGLERS COVE'

It was a warm afternoon in early June when Aireanna and her two brothers Randy and Robbert were with us, their grandparents, and on our sail boat "Endless Summer." We were motoring under power through the last part of the narrow waterway, 'Welcome Passage,' in British Columbia. As we rounded the large rocky point of land at the north end of Welcome Passage, we were all looking for a sign of some kind, that marked the entrance to a Canadian marine park we were seeking named Smugglers Cove.

At my side, Randall was learning to use nautical charts, which are maps of the waterways instead of highways. Ranall was helping me watch for an indication of where the entrance to Smugglers Cove was located according to the chart.

"It must be right around here somewhere Grandpa."

"Your right Randy but all I see are large boulders everywhere."

Aireanna said "Granpa there is some kind of small white thing up on top of that gigantigus rock over there."

"Okay sweetheart remember where you saw that, but I think we'll motor up around that point over there and see if the entrance is around there."

"Robbert will you go forward to the bow and look for rocks or logs under water so we don't hit anything when we get in close, and hang on to the forestay so you won't fall overboard."

"Okay grandpa" he said as he walked up the side deck toward the front of the boat. After rounding the point, nothing seemed to look like an opening of any kind.

"Aireanna. we'll go back to where you saw something, up on top of that rock. Keep an eye out and tell me when you see it again." I said.

It wasn't long before Aireanna's straining eyes found what she was looking for "There it is grandpa up on top of that big rock."

"I see it too " said Robbert.

"Okay we'll go in a little closer. Randy you watch our depth sounder to keep track of much water we have under the boat."

Endless Summer was then turned toward the rocky coastline and as we drew nearer I slowed the engine down to an idle, which just moved us slowly through the water. When we got closer it was easy to see that the little white speck Aireanna had seen was indeed a small sign indicating that this was indeed the entrance to Smugglers cove.

When we were in closer to shore you could only see huge boulders everywhere.

“Grandpa” Robbert said, “It looks like we can get in over there.”

When I looked to where Robbert was pointing, I could see a small channel between the rocks. “Okay lets take a look.” I knew my grandchildren were aware that I had been sailing boats since their own mothers and fathers were children. But I liked teaching them about things, and I felt that giving them responsibilities is good for their personal growth.

With Endless Summer moving at a snails pace, the boat was pointed into the narrow channel of water. Aireanna was helping Robbert look for hidden danger under the water, while Randall was watching the depth sounder and telling me how much water was under the boat every time the depth sounder changed more than a couple of feet.

Robbert said.“grandpa we need to go to the left a little bit, cause there is a big rock under the water right ahead, on our right side, I mean on our Starboard side.”

I was glad it was low tide, because if it had not been low tide they may not have seen that rock and we could possible have hit it with the bottom of the keel which was a little over five feet under the water itself.

Then just as Randy said “we have thirteen feet of water under the boat”

Aireanna said “Grandpa I see a sail boat mast up ahead around those other rocks” This was good news because we were in such a narrow water channel that we couldn’t turn around. If we were to change our minds now it would be necessary to back the boat out of the channel and this would not be an easy task, because boats don’t go backwards very well.

Finally we rounded a small bend in the channel and entered a small but comfortable anchorage. Because of the popularity of places like Smugglers cove in British Columbia it is the custom, that once you have your bow anchor down and set firmly in the sandy bottom, that you also tie a line from the stern of the boat to a tree or rock on the beach to keep your boat in one location. This allows more room for other boats in these small secluded anchorage’s.

After Robbert lowered the anchor to the bottom and I backed the boat up to set the anchor into the sand properly, Randall was rowing the dinghy with Aireanna letting out the stern line as they went toward the shore.

When the dinghy touched the sandy beach Aireanna jumped out with the rope and started to pull. Randy pulled the dinghy up on the beach a little bit then began helping Aireanna when they heard their grandfather call out to them.

“Randy, Aireanna do you see that bright orange spot painted on the rock just in back of you” As soon as he saw it, Randall understood what I wanted him to do. I had told him before that in some state parks the Canadian government had installed mooring rings for boaters to use rather than trees. This was done to protect the trees against damage.

Between the two of them Randy and Aireanna were able to remember how to tie a bowline knot which could be untied easily now matter how hard any thing pulled against it to make it tight. It was one of my favorite knots and I had insisted they learn how to tie it. With the stern of the boat tied to the mooring ring on the rock, they rowed back to the boat and climbed on board.

Once they were back on board the boat, they put up the boom tent, and draped it over the sails main boom, then the boom tent was fastened with lines from the corners of the canvas to different life lines. This shaded the cockpit of the boat from the bright sun or would keep us dry if it rained.

The boys were drinking lemonade that their grandmother had made, and while Aireanna was helping her make home made cinnamon rolls for the evening meal.

As we watched the day end in its yellows, orange and red colors with the sun setting down between the trees on a nearby point of land, Randy asked.

“Grandpa why do they call this Smugglers Cove. Were there pirates or something here? “

“Well I don’t know about pirates, but my understanding is that this place was a hideout for rum runners during the prohibition years in the 1930s. That was when it was against the law to make, or sell, whiskey in the United States.”

“Whats a rum runner grandpa” asked Aireanna.

“A rum runner is a person that smuggled whiskey or another alcohol called rum across the border into the United states or across state lines from one state to another in the United States “ I said.

Robbert was curious and asked “How did they get it there grandpa.”

“Well they probably kept it stored here in a shed, then after dark they would load it into a very fast speed boat and quietly motor out of the cove, and down through Welcome passage and then perhaps a fast run down to Sucia Island in the San Juan Islands of the United states, or maybe somewhere closer. Then they would transfer it to another boat, or maybe row it ashore to a waiting car or truck. Eventually it would end up in a place called a Speakeasy where people would go secretly to buy it and drink it.”

FOGGY BAY

We were returning to San Francisco Bay from a trip we had made to Drakes Bay just a few miles up the California Coast. It was about 12:30 P.M. when we passed under the Golden Gate bridge heading into the Bay itself. The trip down the coast from Drakes Bay had been one in bright warm sunshine, almost to a baking stage of heat.

As we closed in on the San Francisco Bay we encountered a huge wall of very dense fog inside the Bay. Not knowing how far into the bay the fog extended, we set a compass bearing course from our known position at the bridge, and set the course to intersect the number two turning buoy for the ship channel just to the south of Angel island. We also set our automatic fog signal to be sounded at one minute intervals, as required by maritime law, and entered the fog bank.

Even at dead slow speed it seemed like we were going to fast. You could hear fog signals from many distant sources, some were deep throaty moaning voices of the large ships as they moved about. Some were the little beep beep sounds of small boats using the freon gas horns while trying to find their way home to a safe harbor. Ours on "Star Gazer" was electronic, and kind of in between the sound of the multitudes of horns being sounded.

There were four of us aboard, I was at the helm, and the other three were straining their eyes and ears for any thing out of place. At one point, about half way to the number two buoy, Jim said "Don, I hear a fog horn on our starboard side that seems to be getting closer".

We all turned our attention in that direction to listen and look. We sounded our horn intentionally at that time and off to our Starboard came a reply from another unseen vessel. We were traveling so slow I began to wonder if we could get out of the way if some one came bearing down on our beam. The other boat signaled and kept coming, also sounding their horn, as did we.

The other vessel, and ourselves, knew we were very close to each other, and apparently were both being very cautious. All of a sudden we cut through the wake of a passing vessel and we heard her horn, now sounding on the Port side of us, and we never saw the other boat visually.

After what seemed like an eternity we began to hear seals and observed seaweed in the water near the boat. We stopped the boat in the water and listened. Using an old trick, I took our hand bearing compass and looked over the top of it for a bearing toward the sound of the barking seals. We knew from our depth sounder what fathom curve we were on, and we also knew there were normally seals on the rocks on the southern side of Angel island.

We fixed a rough position on our chart of the bay, but we had not heard the bellows horn on the number two turning buoy as yet. From our position we set a course for where the number two buoy should be. Shortly we heard the bell of a buoy, and followed it to it's source, it was the number two turning buoy, but the bell was all you could hear. I called the coast guard and notified them that the bellows on the buoy was not functioning. They thanked us and said they would get a repair crew on it right away.

Most all boaters listen to the emergency channel 16 on their ship board radios, it was but a short time later that we heard a notice to mariners that the horn on number two buoy was inoperative.

From this buoy we took a new heading for Treasure Island, and a small anchoring basin where we intended putting the hook down for the night. The fog was still very thick as we groped our way along the shoreline, then Jim and Margie cried out in alarm as they hollered at me. The two of were looking at a palm tree. You can imagine that if your close enough in thick fog to make out a palm tree, your very close to land as well.

We stopped the boat, and began to back it up slowly. Jim was familiar with the island and said "Don, go to your left a short distance, and we should see a large pier." After we found the pier, we followed the tree tops south until we entered the anchorage area. We found the old mooring buoy left over from the clipper ship air craft that used to fly to various ports worldwide from this very location. They were moored here during the worlds fair in the early 1930's, for show and tell I presume.

We didn't tie up to the mooring buoy because we did not know if using it was permitted as this basin is owned by the military. We dropped our hook on the south side of the basin, and after doing so, all hands went below to get a glass of white wine, and to relax for a few minutes.

Jim and I came back topside to shut the diesel engine off, and to check our position as best we could. When we opened the hatch, and entered the cockpit it was as clear as far as the eye could see. The fog had completely lifted and gone away. We sat looking at the early stars and talking about the trip across the bay that took us over four long hours to complete only to put our anchor down and have it clear off.

STOP ALL ENGINES

During the Korean conflict I found myself stationed aboard one of our small, and few remaining Patrol frigates left in the US Navy. She was one of those old type ships that still had steam engines and boilers, instead of the newer steam turbines. She was one of those ships that you grow proud of no matter how much work it took to keep her running. Yet we, the crew, had come to consider her as close to permanent shore duty as you can get without actually being stationed on the beach. We felt this way because of the amount of time we spent in the repair yard, or the dry docks for repairs of one kind or another. When actually she was just an old worn out ship.

We'd just finished one of our several major over hauls, and taking care of last minute tests, when we received word we were going out to sea for sea trials, which was basically just to test everything to see if it all worked okay. We were never at sea very long, not for any particular reason, it just seemed to work out that way.

On this particular trip no one wanted to go to sea, at least not to my knowledge. You have to understand that to us, the ship was just a place to go to work every day. After all most of us had our personal lives on the beach to take care of, I mean who had time to spend at sea.

We left well before morning light. Steaming out of the Yokusuka Bay, Japan with both boilers on line for a change. This seemed different because as a rule we rarely had both boilers on line at the same time before, and both our engines running like singer sewing machines, but of course we always had both engines running while at sea. I was throttle man of the Port engine, and, I felt responsible for this large piece of machinery. I constantly checked to be sure the oiler ,a new fireman apprentice, was getting oil in every oil cup as we ran along for all our different sea trials.

The oiler also had the responsibility of maintaining clean strainer sponges as needed in the hot tank. The hot tank, which preheats water for the boilers, was a large water tank and covered with a very heavy sheet metal lid. This lid had inspection hatches so that someone could check its condition as needed.

During our sea trials every thing went smoothly, and finally the announcement came, over the Public address system, that sea trials were completed and we would now be taking the sea trial inspection party back to the repair yard. The bridge operated the engine telegraphed system indicating that both engines were to be throttled up to flank speed.

This is full speed, and of course full speed for this old ship wasn't really very fast. Maybe eighteen miles an hour, if my memory serves me right, maybe more. At any rate we knew we were on our way home. The officer of the deck wasn't wasting any time getting us back to the Naval base in Yokusuka.

All hands were very jovial, talking and kidding around. Of course down in an engine room, you can't see where your actually in relationship to land, so its normally a rather dull routine, but not on this day. However, there was a great deal of camaraderie below decks.

In the forward Starboard corner of the engine room, by our coffee
pot, the engineering officer was telling the first class Machinist Mate, who generally ran the engine room, about his hot date for this evening. Everyone was in a mild state of excitement, because every thing had gone so well on this trip, and we were getting back to our ship's berth at Yokusuka early. Myself included.

The maximum speed, generally required, in any harbor is five knots. This is required to prevent excessive wave action and erosion, but we were coming in hot at flank speed. In the engine room we received a signal, on both engine order telegraphs, to reduce speed from flank speed, down to full speed. This order, was acknowledged on both engine telegraph's, by myself and the throttle man on the starboard engine. It was also written down on the engine log books stationed at both engines, and the engines throttle speeds were reduced. Or so everyone thought. After a couple of minutes, we received an engine telegraph signal to reduce engine speed down to two thirds speed. Once again the telegraph was acknowledged, and once again the notation made in the engine's log, and engine throttle's reduced. So we thought. Very quickly there after, we received an engine telegraph signal to reduce both of the engine's speed to one third. All acknowledgments were again, made.

Finally we received a telegraph signal ordering, All engines stop. Once again the acknowledgment's were made. Then abruptly the engine order telegraphs rang up full astern for both engines. Even though it is very unusual to do this, we acknowledged the order, and wrote it down in the engine log books.

It was at this point in time, out of the corner of my eye, I noticed that the Port engine was still running at flank speed ahead, it had never been changed despite the recorded settings and engine telegraph acknowledgments. Without hesitation I reached over, grabbed the engine's reverse gear lever, and struggling, I pulled it toward me to the reverse position. This is not an easy thing to do, as you are supposed to stop an engine completely before you put it in reverse, and not just go straight into reverse.

The engine groaned, and moaned, as she tried to stop, and go into a reverse direction. It was very hard on the engine, but she came to a stop, and instantly was going in reverse, also picking up speed. The noise of the many pumps, propeller shaft main bearings and other steam equipment had covered the noise the engine had made coming to a stop under these trying conditions. No one was the wiser.

Suddenly we received a verbal order from the bride to stop all engines over the speaker system. This announcement got the attention of the engineering officer, still over by the coffee pot, and the first class petty officer. By the time they both reached the engine throttle area, both engines were running in reverse and seemed okay. Myself and the other throttle man were in the process of stopping both engines as we had been instructed.

Suddenly, there was a terrible crashing noise, the ship shuddered, and lurched sideways. We didn't hear any orders to abandon ship, so we were fairly sure we had hit something but were not about to sink. About an hour later, after some minor maneuvering of the ship by a tug boat, we were tied up along side of our flag ship. With a great many questions being asked. It seems we had taken twenty-one feet of paint off our flag ships bow, and rammed the dock. Back into the repair yard it seemed.

No one was allowed to leave the ship for three days as a board of inquiry was convened. No fault was ever found.

Whew!!

SUMMER FUN

"Honey, it seems smoky down here." These are not the words you want to hear, when you're about to embark on your summer cruise.

Lyn and I had been planning this trip for months. We'd arranged to have this entire summer off away from our other life hassles. And, we had found a method of making an income several years ago, when out last child left home, that lets us work winters and play summers.

We'd also found someone to sub-lease our slip for the four months we planned to be away, and he'd already paid his first month's slip rental to our marina office. Our groceries were stored away, and our tanks were topped up, and our book shelves were crammed with books we hadn't read. I had numerous magazine articles to write, and five different books I was presently working on. Our sailboat "ITCHY FEET" was low in the water and we were ready.

Finally the morning arrived, and every thing was in place. I reached down to our instrument panel, turned on our main bilge blower, gave it a few minutes, then cranked over our Atomic four engine. It sputtered briefly, then started. As usual I throttled it back a bit to let the engine warm up slowly.

When I was just about ready, I was going to just go forward and drop our bow line, then walk confidently aft, let our stern line go, and back out of our slip. Instead, my life's partner said those endearing words. "Honey it's smoky down here."

Thinking,"Oh sure." I took my sweet time going below. On arrival I found our main cabin engulfed in a damp smoky haze. The little light went on in my head, and it said. "This is not normal."

I'm sure I set a new record for gaining access to our engine compartment, I lifted the engine cover panel, and I found steam and water everywhere. I actually don't recall, but I may have jumped over our sink console area in getting back topside. The blower stayed on, but the engine's ignition was turned off.

Lyn didn't waste time staying below either, she was topside before I realized she'd gone by me. When the smoke and steam cleared out, the first thing I did was to turn off our through hull fittings.

Then a careful survey of what had happened began. I couldn't find a thing wrong. Of course there was something, but what?

Hesitantly I opened our through hull fitting for the engine cooling water, and asked Lyn to start the engine, but, she should be ready to shut it down again quickly.

Now with every possible entry into our engine compartment open, I told her to start the engine. I myself was laying on the galley floor looking in at the rear of our engine so I could scrutinize any thing that might happen. It was only seconds after the engine started when the problem revealed its sinister behavior. I called out to Lyn, and she shut the engine down. I watched the last of the water seeping out of a very small hole in our exhaust system. It was right at the point where the main engine exhaust pipe entered an elbow, and where the cooling water entered the exhaust system.

"No problem," I thought. I'll simply disconnect the rubber hose that connects our exhaust system to the stand pipe, then remove the incoming cooling water from the engine. However, I didn't have a pipe wrench. Once again,"No problem." I'll just go up to the harbor master's office, borrow a pipe wrench, use the wrench to twist the offending pipe out of its threaded coupling on the engine, and replace it with a new one. We should be ready to go in a couple of hours. Wrong again.

With the pipe wrench in hand I found out there wasn't enough room to swing the long handle easily. "Okay no problem." Well it wasn't easy, but within an hour we had all of our sink plumbing disconnected, the over board drains closed, everything removed from under the sink and placed somewhere else. Even the retaining screws were removed so we could move the whole sink and drain board console out of the way.

The interior of the boat looked like we'd been initiated into the three hundred and sixty degree club, from being rolled by a rogue wave offshore.

Now with some operating room, I adjusted the large pipe wrench to fit this portion of exhaust pipe and pulled on its handle. You got it, nothing happened. Now, I knew there was a problem. Every thing was frozen together with years of rust. Nothing was going to come apart.

So here we were, a leak in our exhaust system that would sink a battle ship in relatively few hours, if the crew could live that long because of carbon monoxide poisoning. A man on his way in his boat, expecting to move into a slip he'd sub leased for four months, and Lyn and I sitting in a boat that was barely a controlled disaster area.

I was faced with removing the entire exhaust system manifold. I would have to take it to a marine machine shop, God only knows where, and have the whole thing rebuilt, using a hefty slice of my summer cruising funds. To top it off, I'd have to anchor out near my own marina while someone else enjoyed my slip. I would be rowing back and forth to get things done.

I did have a hacksaw in my onboard tool box. I took the blade out of the saw, reached into the engine compartment, then reinserted the blade, teeth now turned inward, and the offending exhaust pipe was inside the hacksaw. That is between the blade, whose teeth were now facing in as well, and the hacksaw's back.

It seemed to take forever at such short strokes of some three or four inches at a time, but finally I cut through the exhaust system about two and a half inches from the leaky fitting.

At this point I had no idea how I was going to get it back together. I thought perhaps I can rent a threading tool to cut new threads on the part leading back to the engine and put a new short nipple into a new elbow going in the other direction.

Leaving Lyn on board, I started my search for parts and a thread cutting tool for two and a half inch pipe. I finally found a thread cutting tool, but its handle was so long, I knew I wouldn't have room to use it in my tight engine compartment. I had to find another cure. Being resourceful I thought, "Aha. "No problem."

Consulting the yellow pages, I found what I was looking for. I went to an auto parts store where I found a piece of automobile tail pipe extension, you know the one that goes onto the end of your regular tail pipe, and deflects your exhaust downward. These extensions are two stage swaged fittings. One end is larger than the other, and the larger end was what I needed. Due to price I didn't choose the Chrome plated one, just an ordinary one. It would just slip over the two and a half inch exhaust pipe. With two of these, one for a spare, I also purchased four exhaust pipe clamps. Then I went to a hardware store, and purchased a new pipe elbow and a short pipe nipple, and some pipe tape. I intended to cut the threads off one end leaving a threaded section and a short un-threaded section.

Back on the boat, I cut off one end of pipe nipple, and the exhaust pipe extension I purchased. The assembly went easier than I thought it would. The piece of exhaust pipe acted as a sleeve, and let me butt the rebuilt exhaust system together. It was late by the time we got everything back together, but with two of the clamps holding it all together, we crashed into bed for a nights rest. We slept well. Lyn just seems to trust me in these things, as I'm usually able to come up with solutions.

The next morning with every confidence, we opened our overboard fitting once again, turned on the bilge blower, waited a few minutes, and turned the ignition switch. The engine turned over all right but nothing happened. "Now what." My mind was racing. Our sub-lessor was due in today and here we were.

"Okay think about this. Why won't it start?"

I started by pulling the spark plugs figuring it wouldn't be a bad idea to replace them anyway. As I removed each one, I found they were wet. Then I understood what had happened. The steam and water had even entered our carburetor. I removed the spark arrester from the carburetor and put a finger into it. My finger came out wet. Now Lyn supplied me with strips of cloth, which I inserted into our updraft carburetor with long tweezers, one strip at a time until it was dried out. Then I used Lyn's hair dryer, with its nozzle aimed down into each spark plug hole. Within minutes it had helped dry out the engine's interior.

New spark plugs were installed, and everything buttoned back up. The engine started easily now, and purred like a kitten. Okay it purred like an old cat but it was running okay.

We had a good summer cruise in Canadian waters, visiting places we hadn't been on one of our previous trips to our Northern neighbors. The summer was running out as we cleared customs back into the U.S. at Roche Harbor, on San Juan island. After two days of watching the circus atmosphere of the constant traffic in and out of this unique place, we started toward Lopez sound. Our destination was Hunter Bay. As we passed by the ferry landing at the north end of Lopez Island, our engine began to miss badly. Boat speed dropped of, but with the engine still running we decided to finish the run down to Hunter Bay. After putting the hook down, I began to look into the problem of what was wrong with the atomic four engine. What I found was a blown head gasket, and after the engine had cooled, it couldn't be started again.

It was nine O'clock Saturday morning when I rowed ashore to a private dock in Mud bay. I tied my dinhgy up the dock, and started walking up the street in search of a good Samaritan. I found a gentleman, Mr. Bishop, outside working on his home. He seemed to be the only person awake this time of day in the whole area. I explained my predicament to Mr. Bishop, and that I was trying to find a way of getting to a chandlery Fisherman's bay on the other side of the island. Mr. Bishop said to me, as he reached into his pants pocket,

“Cars out by the garage. It’s to old to steal.” At the chandlery I purchased one of those adjustable outboard motor brackets. When I returned Mr. Bishop’s car to him, he wouldn’t accept any payment of any kind. GOD BLESS YOU AGAIN MR. Bishop.

I always keep an assortment of tools on the boat just in case. Lyn and I were able to bolt the outboard motor bracket onto the stern of our sailboat. Then our outboard motor was moved from its storage area down onto this bracket. We timed our departure from Hunter Bay so that we could ride the outgoing tide out of Lopez Pass, then southerly toward Port Townsend. Figuring that if we did it right, we could pick up the incoming tide to help us in approaching Admiralty Inlet. Of course as we cleared Lopez Pass, there wasn’t a breath of wind from any quarter. The outboard was doing its intended job, but with only six gallons of fuel available for the outboard motor, we were a little apprehensive.

In the distance I could see a tide rips as the water was rushing seaward. By the time we got to Partridge Bank, we were down to two gallons, plus or minus, of fuel left in the outboard motor tank. Then the wind gods smiled and brought a northerly to us. With the main and small working jib up, we sailed smartly into Port Townsend. As it turned out we didn’t make our repairs at Port Townsend, and it took us four days to cover the fifty-seven miles to our home port.

Our sub-lessor had left early so we were able to move right into our own slip. In the long run, with two new head gaskets and the engine's head resurfaced, we put her back together again. Boats are sometimes a problem. You just have to weight the inconveniences against the pleasures. So far with Lyn and I, the pleasures are still winning.

CLEARING CUSTOMS

The first year Lyn and I went to Canada we didn't really know what to expect as we entered Canadian waters. I mean we knew the basics, like flying the Canadian flag on our flag halyard, and we knew we had to clear customs, the converting our US dollars to Canadian dollars, and that we could not carry guns on the boat without a lot of hassle, but other than that we didn't have a clue.

We crossed over the waterway border boundary, and found our way to the Canadian customs dock. We tied up to the dock and then walked up the dock to the customs office. While in the customs office the woman customs officer took care of our basic paper work, then she suggested we go down to the boat. 'Oh, well okay,'

On board the boat she had a quick look around below deck, then we sat in the open cockpit while she asked me more questions. One of those questions was phrased as, "Do you have any spirits aboard?"

My first thought,'Spirits, no, no ghosts.'But fortunately I didn't say this thought out loud, because if I had I would have sounded like the typical tourist that I was. However, once I realized she meant liquor, I did say, "Only enough for my own consumption."

She stopped writing, mulled over the answer I had given her a few seconds, then said. "Okay don't tell me exactly how much you have." From that point we finished going through her check list and she gave us our clearance number to be displayed in the main salon window, then wished us a good time during our visit.

After the young lady left, Lyn said to me, “I can’t believe you got away with that.”

Stumped, I replied, “Got away with what?”

“I think, you’re only allowed to bring in one liter of alcohol per person.”

“Really?”

“Yes, and you have three cases of wine.”

“So, what I told her, was basically true.”

We spent a great three months in Canadian waters, and the people we met and dealt with, were wonderful. It was an Indian Summer so the weather was almost like spending time in a favorite anchorage in the south pacific islands.

Finally, we had to return to US waters, and we had to clear customs coming back over our own border. Our chosen port of entry was Roche Harbor in the San Juan Islands. This is a very busy place and an ideal location if you just want to hang on the hook and watch the action, and there is lots of action that takes place in this basin.

When we entered the harbor, and approached the customs dock, it was full of boats, plus a line of boats waiting to be processed. Without giving it a second thought we just anchored, took our papers and rowed our dinghy into the dock.

We waited patiently while the other boats were being taken care of, then one of the customs men, said, “Can I help you?”

“Sure, we’re here to clear customs.”

He glanced quickly up and down the dock, and seeing no boat, he said. “Where’s your boat?”

I pointed to our vessel, and said, “Anchored right there.”

Perplexed, he answered, “Any particular reason you anchored out instead of coming into the dock?”

“You were too busy, and there wasn’t any room at the dock, so we came ashore in the dink.”

I thought,’Apparently this behavior can be permitted,’ because he had me row back out to the boat and get some oranges that were not marked as ‘Sunkist’ and turn them over to him. After that it was only a matter of routine before we were welcomed home. He did make one final remark, “Normally, in this country, you bring your boat into the customs dock.”

CRUISING, IS IT AREA? OR DISTANCE?

I'm often confused over this term, CRUISING. Because Lyn and I cruised on our sailboat for nine years. We found a way to work during the winter months, which filled our cruising fund, and we saved the summer months for our own boating pleasures.

In all of our cruising, I doubt if we were more than a day, or two, away from a snug marina somewhere. We spent endless days completely by ourselves, no other boats to be seen, nor humans to interrupt our daily lives of doing little to nothing. Reading, making love, drinking a little wine, swimming or walking, and exploring.

I cannot tell you how many miles we put under our keel, I suppose I could figure out a rough estimate, but who cares. We didn't cruise to impress others of our nautical ability. We cruised because we chose too.

We, like so many others we met along our waterway paths, were out to enjoy the good things in life while we could. Though I must admit most of the folks we met were only traveling during their brief summer vacation.

Unlike the majority of the delightful people we met during our nine years of living on board and traveling, we owned our boat. I only mention this because to travel in this manner often requires the need to keep ones living expenses at an absolute minimum.

We were able to do pretty much as we pleased because we didn't have house payments to make, car payments were non-existent, insurance, none. No payments of any kind. During our first summer we started out with six hundred dollars and when we finished the summer, we still had about a hundred and thirty dollars left. We never went hungry, well accept for ice cream, and when we did come across a large grocery store, we pigged out on cookies, and candy. Large supermarkets are a rare find when one is cruising in remote areas.

When we returned to the normal civilization, it was only difficult if we thought we should have visited one more spot somewhere.

BUGS

I never claimed to know much about marine bugs, even when my water line began to rise. When it seemed, on one of my rare visits, that the water line was about three inches higher than it was when I'd left the boat some two years earlier, I figured it was just drying out.

You must understand, I'm not someone to disregard my boat's needs, but the company I worked for at the time sent me to Japan to straighten out some company problems. The problems had turned nasty, but, we'll not go into that. As it was, I was gone just over three years.

I had brought the boat up from the California Delta country, which is inland from San Francisco, with the intention of exploring the Puget sound as well as the San Juan and Gulf Islands. She was an old wooden boat with a soft chine, but in good condition.

Of course I felt bad to have to leave her in the wetter climate of the Northwest without me aboard to care for her, but a living is a living. I did leave a very good top quality thermostat controlled heater aboard to keep her dry inside in my absence.

One week, in late September, Jennifer Dunham the marina manager, called me in Yokusuka. The conversation was brief, but the part that I still remember was when she said. "Mr. Boone, I think you'd better come see this."

I had some off time coming to me, so I caught a flight out the next afternoon. It was two days before I could actually get to the marina, and on arriving I immediately went to the marina office. Jennifer was trying to be gentle with me, but when she said, "A duck flew in one side of your dog house, and out through the other side."

"You mean it broke the windows?"

"No sir. You see the duck was in the water, and someone on another boat scared it. It took off in a frightened hurry, and would have normally just hit your boat, but it didn't. Instead it flew right through the hull."

Now I was concerned. The two of us walked down to the far end of the marina, and to a dock rarely used by anyone else. As we walked out onto the finger pier, I could see the boat, and it looked okay to me. Well except for the hole in the side where the duck had come out. Okay it looked dusty, but the paint looked good. Well it should, I mean I had put eight coats of epoxy paint on the whole boat, including the spars before I had to leave, and those eight coats of paint, as it turned out, were pretty thick.

When I got close, I leaned over to have a close look at the hole, and to say I was surprised, is putting it mildly. The hole had an inner shell, and an outer shell, nothing in-between.

I could see what appeared to be small piles of. . .well Sawdust is what comes to mind, some here and some there.

I was about to climb aboard, when Jennifer said. “Don, maybe you better let an expert have a look at the boat before you go aboard.”

“An expert? What kind of expert?”

“A man who knows about bugs.”

I still didn’t have any idea why she would think of bugs, but the fact of the matter was, it looked like the dog house of my motor sailor was but a shell.

That afternoon, an expert on rare bugs was with me, and he’d spent a couple of hours comparing his findings with one text book after another. During his inspection, I heard him murmur, something like, “Ate the pilot house first, then the coach roof. . . Finally, turning to me, he said, You’ve heard of Polyestermites?”

“Yes, came about in Southern California as I recall.”

“Well, you don’t have ‘em.” The he asked, “You’ve heard of Teredo worms?”

“Yes. They’re a bug that eats wooden boats. Although I thought they were only found in warmer tropical waters, and below the water line?”

"Well, you don't have them either. Nope, what you've got puts them to shame. You've got Califsupermites."

"Calif. . . some kind'a mites?"

"Worse actually. I found remains that indicate you've had generations of them living here for some time."

He went on to explain that my bugs, because they were left unchecked, had eaten my boat from the inside out, and top to bottom. He explained that this kind of termite will not leave a perfectly good meal to go out into wet, damp weather, to chomp on hard wet, damp moss covered trees in the northwest. Well, you get the picture. Why leave a good home if you don't have to.

As I pondered the possible lengthy future stay in the boatyard, he asked. "You mind if I step aboard for a better look around?"

"Humm, oh. . .sure. Go ahead."

As he stepped aboard, the boat listed, and in just seconds, that harsh movement of someone actually moving their weight about on her deck, brought a sound unlike any you've ever heard. Kind of like, Kkkuuussccisshh. With a soft rumble resembling that of an elephant passing slow gas. Mr. Bugat, the expert, hollered as he actually ended up standing on top of the aft section of the keel.

The boat that had been above the water line, now collapsed all around him. It seems that now all I had was a large skiff. Even the spars had been hollow tubes. The only part of the hull still intact was the basic hull from about two inches above the water line, down to the keel. This of course left an engine compartment, and tankage.

It was nearly a week before I found someone willing to take her off my hands. A guy who said he'd make a fishing boat out of her remains. As a final act, I took the owners registration with me when I went down to his marina, and signed it off to him.

I didn't tell him, but while he was signing his name to the paperwork, I swear I saw, through the bottom portion of my glasses, the trifocal lens part, a very small set of scuba tanks and swim fins lying next to a termite hole.

PERFECT PICTURE FISH.

It was one of those perfect afternoons. The sun bearing down on the water just outside the back door, causing diamond patterns to reflect on the ceiling inside of our houseboat. I was sitting under the roof of our covered porch on the back deck enjoying the Sun's warmth while sipping a cool drink, and attempting to read the morning paper.

Our houseboat, built a good many years ago, had some quality logs under her. Of course we'd had her leveled in the water with Styrofoam barrels in a few places over the years. Lyn and I bought the house so we could live on the river, and keep our boat tied to our side deck rather than at some marina that we'd have to drive to each time we wanted to get out onto the water for an evening's sail.

This day however, turned out rather odd. I had a fishing line hanging in the water, not that I was actually fishing mind you, more like drowning bait. I'm not sure why, but for some reason I decided to check my line, and when I tugged at it, it seemed to be really tight. So I pulled it harder, nothing happened. I remember saying, "What the heck."

I had a good grip on the heavy rod and reel, so I moved to the south end of the deck, and pulled again. It did move slightly, but only enough to place some encouragement in my psyche. Now I moved to the north end of the deck, a total of nearly thirty feet, and again pulled on the line.

Perhaps I should explain my kind of fishing. I'm not one to use four pound test line and then brag about the size of the fish I caught on it, no way, if I catch a fish I'm keeping it. With this in mind, you'll understand why I use fifty pound test line on my fishing reel.

Okay, let's cut to the chase here. I pulled that damn line continually, and slowly it was reeling in, ever so slowly but I was getting line back onto the reel. I figured I'd actually hooked onto a small log on the river bottom, but I wanted my line back.

One of my neighbors, Mickey, who lives in the houseboat next to mine, came along just as I was struggling with hauling the line in. As Mickey and I often share a glass of something cool while we fix the world, he felt comfortable coming aboard without asking first. "What're you doin." He asked.

"I'm just trying to get my line and hook back, but it's stuck on something."

I no sooner got that said, when the two of us could see something getting close to the surface. Neither of us could believe our eyes. This had to be the biggest fish either of us had ever seen. I still don't even know to this day what it was, other than large. As the Mickey and I wrestled with this huge fish, another neighbor happened by, and he too began to help us get that fish out of the water and up on the back deck of my houseboat.

When finally we were successful, but we wanted to know how much the fish weighed just to satisfy our curiosity. I didn't have a scales at all and the one Mickey had, was not even going to come close to doing the job.

Lyn, who had been sitting in the house reading, started calling fishing friends in search of a larger weight scales to weigh this monster. It wasn't long before a small crowd of men were gathered around looking at this oddity.

Well, in the long run, we couldn't locate a scales big enough in the neighborhood to weigh the fish, so I just took a good picture. Now, to give you an idea of the size of this fish, the picture weighed thirty eight pounds.

IFPublications
mgn.editor@gmail.com

Other books written by Donald Boone

WELCOME ABOARD
When those who have lived around the water, and their day comes to an end, it is time to relax. Whether they are lying in a Vee birth, or on a cushion in the cockpit of a boat. Perhaps even a bed ashore. It doesn't matter as they frequently have an abundance of time. To fill the time they read and let the stories unfold in their mind's as the hours pass by. This book is comprised of stories that take place in this world. A place where you meet life on its terms.
ISBN 1-882896-03-3
EAN 978-1-882896-03-5

CHOOSING LOVERS
Why spend years with the wrong lover.
Find the one that best suits your needs
and enjoy freedom from sexual hunger.
ISBN 1-882896-04-1
EAN 978-1-882896-04-2

CYCLES & RHYTHMS of INTRIGUE
Most of life, if not all of it, contains cycles.
From the birth of any event it will find
its natural rhythm and follow it to the
end. Is life fated, read the answer in this
book.
ISBN 1-882896-07-6
EAN 978-1-882896-07-3

THE CHESS COACH
Becoming one is easy, and it can be very rewarding. If you play the game and have time on your hands, consider becoming a chess coach.
ISBN 1-882896-08-4
EAN 978-1882896-08-0

THE SEA PILOT
In this age of sailing vessels, we no longer fear sailing over the edge of the flat world, and we find our way with compass and chronometer. This was not so when this story took place.
ISBN 1-882896-09-2
EAN 978-1-882896-09-7

CHESS STORIES THROUGH THE AGES
This book, 'Chess Stories Through The Ages,' contains stories that have been passed from one generation to the next down through history. From why 'White moves first, and an unknown story of 'Helen of Troy, found in, 'The Sacrificed Trojan Horse.'
ISBN 1-882896-10-6
EAN 978-1882896-10-3

THOSE WHO PLAY CHESS
Knowing how your opponent plays chess, his or her favorite pieces and their quirks, are a definite advantage to you in this game. Especially if you play in tournaments. This book will provide you with information on them as individuals, and that of their personalities. You will also find lists of historical players with the same kinds of individualism's and personalities to help guide you in your defense at the table.
ISBN 1-882896-11-4
EAN 978 -1-882896 -11-0

IMPACT

Meteors have been haunting mankind since the beginning of mankind, and they still do. This story is about one of those celestial bodies that does not miss the earth on its path around our sun. Like meteorites of the past, the damage it causes when it strikes the earths surface, is devastating. However, many survive and this story is about how one group came together to get through the worst of the affects.

ISBN 1-882896-12-2
EAN 978-1-882896-12-7

THE CHESS GAME

Having lost a huge sum in prize money due to an oversight in a championship chess game, he became a revenge killer. He spelled it out for his opponents during his killing spree. You will see the connection as you read this story.

ISBN 1-882896-13-0
EAN 978-1882896-13-4

www.ingramcontent.com/pod-product-compliance
Lightning Source LLC
LaVergne TN
LVHW010058110826
845155LV00028B/392

* 9 7 8 1 8 8 2 8 9 6 0 3 5 *